TALES OF THE FORGOTTEN GOD
BY DAN HAMILTON

THE BEGGAR KING
THE CHAMELEON LADY
THE EVERLASTING CHILD

TALES OF THE FORGOTTEN GOD

THE CHAMELEON LADY

Dan Hamilton

Illustrated by
Jack Stockman

INTERVARSITY PRESS
DOWNERS GROVE, ILLINOIS 60515

InterVarsity Press® is the book-publishing division of InterVarsity Christian Fellowship®, a student
movement active on campus at hundreds of universities, colleges and schools of nursing in the United
States of America, and a member movement of the International Fellowship of Evangelical Students. For
information about local and regional activities, write Public Relations Dept., InterVarsity Christian
Fellowship, 6400 Schroeder Rd., P.O. Box 7895, Madison, WI 53707-7895.

Cover art: Jack Stockman
ISBN 0-8308-1672-0

Printed in the United States of America ∞

Library of Congress Cataloging-in-Publication Data

Hamilton, Dan.
    The chameleon lady/Dan Hamilton; illustrated by Jack Stockman.
      p.   cm.—(Tales of the forgotten God)
    ISBN 0-8308-1672-0
    1. Fantastic fiction, American.   2. Christian fiction, American.
I. Title. II. Series: Hamilton, Dan. Tales of the forgotten God.
PS3558.A4248C48   1994
813'.54—dc20   94-16541
                                  CIP

17	16	15	14	13	12	11	10	9	8	7	6	5	4	3	2	1
08	07	06	05	04	03	02	01	00	99	98	97	96	95	94		

For Jennifer Elise Hamilton—
daughter, friend-in-miniature,
beloved shadow, and future lady

—CONTENTS—

—PREFACE—

Once there was a City where dwelt the Elder God and the men and women and animals and wonders he had made. All shone, all had joy, and all were loved.

But there were ways to leave the City—paths that were still forbidden to the people though left open to their feet, avenues made not by the Elder God, but by his old enemy who hated good things everywhere. All that the people needed was given them freely, but they were not content as long as the untrodden paths to the unexplored wilderness shimmered in the sun. So they left one day, first by ones, and then by groups, until they had all left the City to see what lay beyond. The Elder God called after them all, but curiosity deafened them and stopped their ears.

First the wilderness lay before them, then beside them on either hand, and then it surrounded them. And the wilderness terrified them, for there were lions there, and wolves, and fierce things that lived in the sea. Darkness fell upon them, and rain and thunder—the sad voice and tears of the Elder God. The world was changed in a great shaking and windstorm; the people turned, but could not find the way back to the City. And too late they understood that the roads would have been theirs to explore, and the wonders beyond theirs to conquer, had they waited until they had been tested, approved and empowered. Instead, they went in their own strength to conquer the wilderness, and it was the wilderness which conquered them.

The City was never lost; it was only removed from the face of the earth and still was—somewhere. But the people were lost, and it was the path back to the City that was forfeit.

The people made themselves a king to remind them of the Elder God, but no man falsely exalted could truly fill the empty throne. The people built Glory where they believed the city had been, but it was only a wicked and flimsy shadow. Some thought there might still be a secret door, and behind it a dark and dangerous path to the City, winding its way back if only one could plumb its mysteries. But if there was a door leading to such a path, it was hidden, and no one knew where it was. Each year fewer searched for the fabled door, and then the people lost count of the years. Glory endured and they still crowned kings, but the memory of the Elder God largely faded from the land. In few places was he still worshiped; in no place was he altogether without a witness.

And then the beggar came. Covenant. The beggar who reigned as a quiet king. The dusty man who spoke for the Elder God and changed lives around him frequently and forever. The one who bent the twisted world around him so that those who stood with him could see its true shape. The man who raised the dead to life again and granted rest to the bone-weary. The traveler who defeated fire and fired the defeated to new heights of courage and honor. The patient man who sifted the refuse of the world and recovered men and women and children (and even animals) and made them whole again in the midst of their imperfections.

Those he redeemed he called to his house in Glory. The old stone ruin was weathered and unremarkable from the outside, but on the inside it was a wonderful warren of comfortable rooms and kitchens and places to meet and eat and heal. And behind one particular door lay the path to the City.

The City is still the center of all the universe—it is there that the Elder God reigns in unapproachable holiness. The City has a heart and a name, and that same heart beats at the core of the earth and clocks the candling of the stars.

This part of the story was told in *The Beggar King*.

ONE

The Face
in the
Shadows

WORDSMITH GRASPED BEAUTY'S ARM AND POINTED through one of the tower windows. "Watch—there, in the street below us."

She looked and saw nothing.

"In the shadows," he continued. "I think she is coming here."

"She?"

"I saw her face in the moonlight just now."

"Who is she?"

"I do not *know*," he said uncertainly.

"Who do you *think* it was?" Beauty asked.

"A woman dead many years," he answered quietly.

She dared say nothing. *Anything is possible in this house*, she thought. *Anything.*

They both gazed down, where the woman was only a shadow in the dimly lit streets of Glory. Unheeded in the darkness, she wound her way to the gray stone house where the door was never locked.

A moment later they heard the ghost echoes of a knock. Binder appeared from the corridor and opened the door; he was already drawing the woman into the candlelit front hall as Beauty and Wordsmith approached. The woman looked up at them, and Beauty gasped. All their eyes fixed themselves upon the stranger's face.

"So I remind you of someone?" the newcomer asked softly.

"Yes," said Wordsmith.

"Yes," said Binder.

"Yes," said Beauty.

"Who, then?" she challenged gently.

"A woman from a long time past," answered Wordsmith.

"A girl I knew in days before," said Binder.

"A child I used to play with," said Beauty.

"Then tell me the color of my hair, and my height, and the shade of my eyes," she said.

"You are tall," said Wordsmith, "with long black hair and dark blue eyes."

Beauty looked at him with widened eyes. "What are you saying? Her hair is red, and her eyes are green, and she is the size of a mere child."

"You are both wrong," said Binder. "Her hair is the color of the sun, and her eyes are brown, and she is my height less an inch."

The woman smiled sadly. "You see?" she said. "I am the Chameleon Lady—my image lies solely in the eye of the beholder.

"What am I wearing?" she continued.

"A cloak the color of the doves that flutter in the dust," answered Beauty promptly, "with purple piping and a purple lizard embroidered upon the collar."

Wordsmith nodded as Binder spoke his agreement.

"You see?" she said. "My cloak remains the same, but the rest of me is ever shifting."

"Then who *are* you? What *do* you look like?" asked Beauty.

"I no longer know," said the stranger. "My mirror lies even to me."

Beauty looked thoughtfully at Wordsmith. "There is a mirror in this house that does not lie," she said.

Beauty drew the woman after her along the hall and stopped before a large mirror mounted on the wall.

"See here," she pointed. "This is a magic mirror."

"I have had more than enough of magic," moaned the newcomer. She shrank back from the mirror and would not open her eyes to it.

So Beauty looked instead—and saw nothing, not even herself in the depths of the mirror. The silver that ever shimmered was now lifeless and still.

Wordsmith, standing behind them, said quietly, "This mirror never lies. But it does not always speak." He faced the strange woman squarely. "I think you should abide here until Covenant returns. Though the key to some of its secrets has been trusted to my hands, this is his house, and a mystery too deep for his mirror will not be too deep for him."

"Thank you," she said. "I came here because I heard that this door is never locked and there are always kind words in abundance."

"That is our task," he said, "and our joy as well."

"And I have also heard of a beggar," she added.

"You have, and he is Covenant, and he is real, and he is the heartbeat of this house. The question is not how we will treat you, but what Covenant will do with you. We are only human; though we have learned not to decide too quickly, even our opinions in the end mean little. Covenant's judgments are lasting and leave no room for argument."

"And who," murmured Beauty, "would argue with mercy?

"Come with me," she continued in a louder but still kind

voice, "and I will find for you a bed."

Wordsmith smiled to himself, remembering the night he had spoken those same words to a lost and voiceless Beauty. Now she was in turn extending that kindness to another, and the circle of compassion had completed another turn.

"You will need help," Binder said. "I will send Flamerider and Firecolt to warm and fill a bath for you."

Wordsmith, knowing all things were well in hand, ascended to his study and turned his pen to paper again.

The first vision of this night has come true already, he thought. *Now I have seen the woman without a face. Or does she have too many faces?*

The crown of the old stone house in Glory was Wordsmith's tower, a room with four windows that looked out over Glory and beyond, and a fifth window that opened upon somewhere altogether different. Beyond that pane were constellations and whirling planets, darkness and intricate patterns, subtle plays of light and shadow that either were stories themselves or triggered tales in the mind of the watcher. Wordsmith sat before the window and saw the things that unfolded there, and hunched over paper in the mostly magical and faintly futile attempt to record the dreams and visions of the night.

This deep into the hours of darkness there was no other motion elsewhere in the house. The only two awake were in the tower now, as Beauty ascended the familiar winding stairs and came to the secluded room. She stepped softly behind Wordsmith, thinking him unaware of her arrival. But without taking his eyes from the swirls and stars that shimmered in the fifth window, he reached out his hand for hers. She took it silently, and their fingers spoke for them, and the warmth of each renewed the other.

Their entwined fingers mirrored the joined pledges on the chains about their necks. She had made her promise to stay with him, and he with her, and the metal of promise was a comfortable burden that each shouldered well.

The words of Covenant still echoed in Beauty's ears, joining them together in both time and eternity. Still it was a wonder to her, that of all the men she had known she should be united with the one man who had shown her the most kindness, who had been drawn to her not by her great beauty and former fame but by her poverty, isolation and suffering. He had not demanded her love as a price for his own care, but had accepted her as a prize won by his care for her, and had taken her needs as his own.

Covenant's care was at the core, for Covenant—the beggar—had changed their lives. They thought often of the strange and splendid man who had burst into their lives to bring them to this house in Glory and together.

Wordsmith once was a drunken bard, bitter with the taste of a crippled leg and the weight of failed dreams. Now he stayed up with the stars and wrote down visions and truths, copying them in books to sell in the marketplace to anyone who would buy.

Once the fairest flower of Glory, Beauty had been left behind by fame in the drift of time. Once all men had been hers, and she was never content. Now, only one man sought her love, and she was more than satisfied.

Wordsmith had then been named steward of the House of Covenant. But his first place was still before the windows, and Beauty was content to join him there. Indeed, she knew no reason to leave his side for long. Many had joined the fellowship at the House of Covenant, and now other hands did the main work of laying the Feast daily for the homeless and the hungry and all who would come to the rebuilt ruin in the back alleys of Glory.

"What have you seen tonight?" Beauty asked her husband.

"Little that I can make sense of," Wordsmith answered. "Many strange things that I wish Covenant were here to explain. I have seen an ancient book with a sword growing from its pages, while a young man pores over the words and his spirit blazes within him. I have seen a woman with no face riding a lizard. And I have seen a man in chains suddenly sprouting wings and clawing his way upward across the rocks."

"Your dreams are always strange," she said. "But they always mean something, and we have seen the lady with no face riding her curse."

Wordsmith nodded.

"Where is Covenant?" she asked. "And how long will he be gone? He has not been here for days."

"I have seen him, too," he answered. "He is a long way from Glory."

"Has Lionheart left as well? I saw him early tonight buttoning his cloak in the hall."

"Yes. He has far to ride tonight."

"How swift are his beasts? I have never seen them running."

"Swifter than horses, and always fast enough. I watched him in the glass as he left," he said, gesturing to the window that overlooked the west edge of Glory. *I am always thrilled when they come to his call*, he thought. *Nothing can be seen in the trees until he roars, and then at his voice the lions are suddenly there.*

Wordsmith was unsure they were always the same ones, though there generally seemed to be two—a great male and a smaller female. Lionheart said he often rode the female while the male ranged ahead and beside them as a guard. "But when speed is more useful than caution," Lionheart had said, "I ride with my face in his mane, and we outrun the wind."

Though Wordsmith could see many things at a great distance through the magically magnified windows, he could not see where the sun did not reach. He saw very little of Lionheart's nocturnal doings and did not understand how Lionheart knew when to go and where to seek. But go he did, and the more intimate secrets of his calling remained between himself and Covenant.

"He should be home soon," said Wordsmith. "Shall we go down and meet him?"

They descended and were met in the front corridor by a roar of laughter that lightened the house. Lionheart still carried the tang of a wild animal; Wordsmith could not guess how many leagues he had ridden that night in rescue.

But Lionheart held two infants in his arms, and close behind him tottered an old man nearly blind with age and withered with weakness.

"Good hunting?" asked Wordsmith, more as a ritual than a question.

"Very good hunting," answered Lionheart, brushing back his great mane of hair and shaking the weight of the night from his weary shoulders. "But then it is easy to pluck the fruits that are left unwanted in the orchard."

He moved away down the hall, the old man clinging to his belt for guidance and support.

* * *

All those in Covenant's house heard the strange lady's story the next morning.

"What is this curse upon you?" asked Beauty gently. "We have seen many remarkable things here in this house, and this must be numbered among them."

"It is the curse of the chameleon," she began. "I have sewn the figure of a small lizard on my collar, and I am burdened with a necklace fashioned in the shape of a chameleon. I do not know who I really am."

"Why is your necklace a burden? Can you not take it off?"

"This necklace will never come off," she said. "And even if I could take it off, I would die. So runs the curse."

"What is this curse?" Beauty asked again. While she alone was speaking, Wordsmith, Binder and the rest waited for the stranger's answers.

She sighed and began an old tale many times told, and no less painful for its familiarity.

"I deceived a man, and he cursed me, and his words came true."

Beauty reached for her hand. "I, too, have suffered from the words of men—and their deeds."

"But did their curses ever come true?" Something blazed in the woman's eyes for a moment and then died down again.

"It was not their curses that came true," Beauty said evenly, "but their blessings that were false. Many men praised me, honored me, showered promises upon me and adored me, but none of it was of any value in the end. Their loyalty failed, and they turned their attentions to another who had not yet been ravaged by time." Beauty's voice softened. "But that is a tale for another day, and I will not interrupt you again."

The newcomer stared at the wall for a long moment before resuming. "I had a sister whose lover would often come to her by night and meet her in her darkened room.

"My sister was beautiful, and I was not. One night I tricked her into seeking elsewhere for her lover, and I hid myself in her unlit room to wait. There he came to me, through the window; he slipped this pledge around my neck, and we said nothing, letting our passion speak for us. But he soon realized the deception, and he lit the lamp and beat me and cursed me.

"My sister called him a 'magic man,' and so he was. I learned too late that he could throw spells and do dread deeds with a power I could not understand."

"Perhaps he was a servant of Fame," Wordsmith suggested. "Fame may be false to the very core, but he is not without power and gifts to those who follow him."

"Whoever he is, he turned this necklace into a pledge of punishment. My sister found me and cursed me as well. She drove me out and left me friendless and homeless. I have drifted through Glory and the land around ever since."

"Is there any way to break the curse?" asked Wordsmith.

"Her magic man said that there was a cure for the chameleon curse," she answered, "but that another man of power would have to pay the price himself. He said that I would never find one who both could and would make me whole again."

Even as Wordsmith gazed, her image slowly changed from one old memory into another. She glanced up at him and smiled wearily. "I know that look," she said. "Another memory. Each time you see me I am different, both strange and familiar at once. Everyone remembers me, but no one knows what I look like."

He could see the bond forming between Beauty and the Chameleon Lady. *I know what it is,* thought Wordsmith. *Both of them have been trapped behind their faces, prisoners of others' ideas of beauty. Covenant set my lady free and gave her to me, but what of this one? Who is she, and what can be done for her?*

Her face dissolved and rearranged again as she fingered the embroidered design on her cloak: a purple chameleon turning tightly in the confines of a black square. "It can't find its way out," she said sadly. "I saw the design in an old book, and I thought it true enough to bear as my own mark. This is how people know who I am. You cannot describe my face and stature so that anyone will recognize me, so perhaps you should continue to call me as I have called myself—the Chameleon Lady."

"With any shape, behind any face, you are welcome to stay here," said Wordsmith. "I am the steward of this house, but the true master is away. When he returns, you should meet him and tell him your story."

"But do not be surprised if he knows it already," cautioned Binder.

"No one will ridicule you here," added Beauty. "We have all borne our share of sorrows, and we have no wish to add to your burdens. Come and go as you please. Though we will know you by the device of the chameleon, we will not use that name for you if you wish it."

"Then what will you call me?"

"Perhaps," said Binder, "we should simply call you our friend. When Covenant returns, he will no doubt have a better name at hand."

"That seems to be his specialty," added Beauty.

"Where did Covenant come from?" the Chameleon Lady asked.

"Even that we don't know," admitted Wordsmith. "Trueteller was the first of us to meet him, but even then she had heard rumors about a man who gave away gold and raised the dead to life again."

"The beggar?" Her eyes widened. "I have heard of him. And before that?"

"Nothing that I can discover. He has merely appeared among us, as though he has come a long way for a purpose he will not yet reveal."

"How old is he?"

"I don't know if age is even a proper term to lay upon him. I often wonder if he was ever born, and I am convinced he will never grow old and feeble. How can we know? No one has ever come to us from the Elder God before. We have no standard to measure him against."

TWO

The
Black
Banner

Leagues away from glory, in the long shadow of the afternoon, the fishing fleet returned to the weathered village of Graycove. A gathering of salt-battered houses and open fishing sheds clung to the rocks and the sand by the untracked ocean, where two separate domains collided. These people were bound to the sea, but bound by the land—of the sea but not on it, and on the land but not in it. Had the waves been solid enough, they would have built their homes on the foam.

Each boat in the oncoming flotilla bore its share of the harvest of the waters, with bright flags atop the masts signaling a good catch. The brighter the flags, and the more of them flying, the better and more valuable the catch aboard. At the rough wooden pier, men, horses and wagons waited impatiently to buy and carry. The fish would be sorted, haggled over, paid for and packed in cold wet seaweed for the long journey to Glory.

Women gathered on the shore and chattered excitedly as they numbered the boats and their banners, but they suddenly stilled when they spotted the last boat, trailing the others by a few hundred yards. No bright flag flew upon it, only a single midnight slash of fabric. One waiting woman recognized the *Childsbreath* and uttered her name aloud. The others echoed the name in whispers, and two of their number began to cry—the half wail that is born in sudden fear and is fully loosed only when dark suspicion is confirmed as truth.

Unwatched now, the other boats passed by the women; the trailing boat drew onto the sloping sand, coming ashore directly before the village and away from the fishing sheds. A tall fisherman splashed down from the deck and gently hoisted the body of a boy to the sand, while another man stood silent in the shadow of the sail.

"He fell into the water," the fisherman said into the breathless hush, "and was caught in the nets. He drowned before we could fight to him and cut him free."

For one woman, grieving began in earnest. The others helped her cry.

The boat did not linger on the sand. "There are a few fish to sell," the fisherman said, "and the buyers are waiting. He caught a net full of fine fish before he died, and I cannot allow his labors to be wasted." He waved to the man still on board, who turned the *Childsbreath* about and set after the other boats.

Soon the rest of the women drifted away to their own men in their own boats and to the fish they might yet redeem from the bargaining pile. Only three, and those beyond speech, were left on the sand. The fisherman stood stiffly in the breeze; tall and lean, the salt winds had long since scoured away any extra weight, and the sun had burnished his skin like old leather. His wife, short and lean, whittled by worry and trimmed by toil, cradled the body of her boy in her arms, rocking him as though he were once again the infant in need of comfort. Her sobs were echoed by the keening of the gulls overhead.

And then the beggar came to them, and they were no longer alone. Where there had been sand and silence, there was now an unobtrusive presence beside them. He was an unremarkable beggar in a dusty brown cloak of many patches. He was neither old nor young, short nor tall, but the traces of countless miles were plain on his countenance.

The beggar reached down and boldly stroked the dead boy's hand. "He is only asleep, you understand. This kind of death is not forever."

The fisherman turned to the beggar with an angry fist clenched tightly at his side. "What *kind* of death?" he challenged. "Death is *death!* Do you not know it even when he gapes before your eyes?"

The woman said nothing, only crying softly and gripping her boy, and staring out at the sea, her endless, eternal enemy: strong, unbeaten and ever hungry.

"I know your mind," the beggar said softly to the woman, ignoring the man and his anger for the moment. "No enemy is truly eternal, though it may seem endless. It is one thing to be undefeated, and another thing entirely to be undefeatable. Perhaps in the end you shall see this ocean burn."

The beggar shifted his stance, and the fisherman saw his face clearly for the first time.

"You!" he exclaimed, and then his voice dropped to a whisper. "Your face has haunted my dreams."

The beggar peered intently into the eyes above his own. "You have seen me many times when your eyes were closed. Open your eyes now, and behold me in person!"

"Who are you?" he asked uneasily.

"Who did you expect from your dreams?" countered the beggar. "Did not the man who haunts your dreams come with a message from the Elder God?"

"Then you came with lightning and with power," he replied, "but I see now you are no strong man."

"Strength can be measured in many ways," the beggar answered, a smile playing at the corners of his mouth. "Miracles do not depend upon muscle but on a higher might."

"A miracle? You are too late. I sought a miracle this morning."

"You will have more than your fill this evening."

"And what is the name of the man who makes me this promise?"

"There is more than one answer to that question," replied the beggar, "for names are a subtle business. Perhaps it is best if you call me Covenant; for I am a man of many words, and all of them are true. I give promises, and then I keep them."

"I am Seareaper," said the rugged fisherman, more gently now. "My wife is Wavewatcher. The boy is—was—Foamrider." The beggar only nodded, as though hearing old facts confirmed. "He had only us, and we had only him."

"And now you are desolate?"

"No! I will wrest from the sea its treasure, as I always have!" he shouted fiercely, gesturing at the dark water with clawed hands. He had finished his crying already, through the long day at sea, but his anger still burned in the approaching dusk. He was thinking of the treasures he had already given in exchange.

"The ocean and I are old enemies," he continued, watching the restless waves vent their energy on the sand. "My brother, too, was taken by the sea. He, and our father before us and my wife's father before her." He turned to Covenant. "The sea is not a kind companion."

"Many things are your enemy in this world," said the beggar, "but not the one who stands before you. My name is Covenant, and I practice the impossible. Do you dare to hope in your darkness?"

Seareaper remained silent, and spoke for his wife as well.

"I did not think you would," continued Covenant. "I know you to be a skeptical man, who believes in nothing that he cannot see or taste or hold in his hands. I have come to change that. I bring you a challenge," he said. "Give me your boat, and I shall give you back your boy."

Wavewatcher could stand their conversation no more; she stood with her boy's body in her arms and began walking wearily toward the village. Seareaper watched her tenderly, but could find nothing to say to her.

When she was many yards away, the fisherman laughed sadly and turned to mock the beggar. "I have lost my boy. Must I lose my boat as well? Get out of here," he said bitterly. "We have little use for those who do not earn their keep."

"I may or may not be a beggar. Is he a beggar who owns everything and keeps nothing? Trade me your boat for your boy," he repeated, not mockingly but as one issuing a dare. "Someday, I shall have a voyage to make from these coasts."

Seareaper stared out to sea and answered with defeat ringing hollowly in his voice. "Why not? I can always build another boat." He gazed after his wife fondly but sadly. "And we are too old to build another boy."

"Then let us go aboard the *Childsbreath*, you and I," suggested the beggar. "She is a chosen vessel and may show us a wonder or two."

Curiosity and grief tumbling in his heart, Seareaper began to scrape his tired body across the sand to the crowded pier, bustling with buying and business. The beggar followed but did not cease his questions as they walked. "Names are important. Tell me where *Childsbreath* comes from," he prompted.

"You seem to know everything; you should know that as well."

"I know that your boat has both an unusual name and a figurehead," said Covenant. "The others have only names, and those more common."

They could see the figurehead clearly now, the wooden image of a child with compelling eyes and outstretched arms.

"I carved it myself," said Seareaper, "for I could describe it for no one else to carve. Only my mind's eye saw it well, and even so this is a faint wooden reflection. I have seen it only in my dreams, but then many times. I would know the child if I saw him."

"And the name?"

"*Childsbreath* because this tiny child in my dreams came to me and breathed on me gently. His breath was very, very sweet and left me aching and fulfilled at the same time."

They began to wade from the shore into the shallow water. Most of the boats had unloaded now, and only one other boat remained at the pier in front of them.

"Why do you ask these questions?" queried Seareaper. "You are only playing with me, for you know the answers already."

"I do, but it is you who must voice the answers aloud."

"You were in those dreams as well. I saw you standing together."

They reached the *Childsbreath* and clambered aboard.

"Go on home," Seareaper said to his friend at the tiller. "The hard part is done."

The friend departed, and Seareaper turned his eyes ahead.

Riding high and light now in the water, the last boat before them eddied away from the uneven pier into the harbor. There were still five empty wagons, with impatient and frustrated buyers, each envisioning a wasted night and day before the empty boats could go and return laden.

"So few fish," Seareaper muttered, "compared to the other catches. It hardly seems worth selling them now. Perhaps I should keep them and dry them for another time."

"Fish do not keep well," said the beggar. "They were never intended to leave the sea. You would be better served to sell them to those who would buy, or, better yet, to give them away to those who cannot buy." He gestured to a ragged company of women and children who stood forlornly a few paces from the wagons. "There are hungry people in your village. Why do you not feed them first?"

"The buyers have more money," replied Seareaper curtly. "As always, those with no money may have the fish worth the fee." He pointed further along the shoreline, downwind from the village, where long-winged gulls wheeled over piles of dead and rotting fish—bony fish, gnarled with impossible scales or filled with poison and agony, discarded for the birds and the poor to pick over. "All the spoils of the sea go to Glory," he said bitterly. "We keep only what they do not buy and need not be left for the scavengers."

"Have you any fish?" One of the fishmongers called from beside his wagon.

"A few," Seareaper called back disconsolately, readying a hawser to be tossed ashore.

"I'll buy all you have," said the man as he grabbed the rope and made it fast to the pier. "High prices for good fish!"

Seareaper looked down at the few dozen fish heaped in the bottom of the boat. "It won't take long to load them," he said only to himself and the following breeze. "Or much money to buy them."

He was wrong. He unloaded fish from the boat onto the buyer's scales until the wagon was piled high and deep and his back ached. Each time he reached in for what must surely be the last fish, he felt three more beneath his groping fingers.

The sun slid further and further down the sky, but still there were fish in the boat. One fishmonger had already tired of the wait and gone away for the night. The remaining three buyers vied for the fisherman's attention and succeeded; Seareaper's final fish filled the final wagon, and the *Childsbreath* rode like a feather at the empty pier. The wagons creaked away behind a storm of curses, and there were none left on the pier save a few ever-hopeful beggars and a handful of men who had heard of the miracle of the fish. Seareaper counted the coins cupped in his hands and would not look at Covenant.

"Why is there more money here in my hand than was paid me? Another one of your tricks?"

"Perhaps. There were those in the wagons who weighed with light scales and paid with lighter coins. I do not think they will all profit from their unworthy trade," said Covenant. "Tomorrow's wind may be ripe with the reek of rotting fish on the road to Glory."

"This is a miracle, but it is a miracle that cannot heal tragedy. It is still blood money! Take it! I cannot keep this in exchange for my own flesh!"

Covenant shook his head.

Seareaper clutched only what the fish were worth in his eyes and scattered the rest of the coppers to the ring of hungry and puzzled watchers. "Then *you* take it! I cannot keep blood money!"

They scrambled for the coins even as other villagers arrived. Word of the miracle of the fishes had spread quickly, and news of the overflowing coppers was soon added to the rumors.

"Would you see another miracle?" the beggar called to the gathering people, although Seareaper saw the beggar's eyes fixed on him alone. "All you who caught no coins, go to the place of the worthless fish and gather all that you can. Those fish may be despised and discarded, but they shall not be worthless to you. Each of you take as many fish as you can carry in your baskets. Take everything—the meatless, the poisonous, the disgusting. Bring them back here, all of you, and I will show you a third miracle."

A very few went. Some laughed openly. The rest made no motion at all.

Not knowing what else to do, Seareaper huddled at the bow of the *Childsbreath* and cradled his head in his arms.

Everyone waited for a spectacle, some less patiently than others, and they were not disappointed. When the desperate few returned with the long-dead fish, the stench came with them.

"Their reek rises to the heavens," grumbled Seareaper.

"They were not meant to rot," Covenant answered, "for they were never meant to die." He gestured at the ancient graveyard further up the hill. "Nor were they. And the day shall come when they will never be dead again."

Seareaper's response burst from him unchecked even by politeness now. "First you talk of death that isn't, and now you give us this: a parade of fools, worthless men bearing even more worthless fish! You laughed at death while we cried, and now you are solemn while we laugh at you! You do not fit in this world."

"Perhaps it is this world which no longer fits around me. As for worth, it is not your task to assign value to men." Then Covenant spoke to a boy standing close before him, holding a long-dead fish at arm's length. "Open its mouth," he commanded. The boy did, and shook a copper coin out into his hand. The rest pried dead jaws apart and found similar gifts. Murmurs exploded into a riot of sound.

One family, who had gone with more children and so carried back more fish, poured their copper coins together in a jingling mass. Other villagers ran to rummage and dispute over the distant piles of discarded fish, looking for more coins that were not there. It was far too late for them. They found no coppers, no wondrous fish, only smell and stench and rotten meat and decay that would not easily wash away.

Covenant spoke again to the boy, still standing open-mouthed before him on the pier. "Now throw your fish back into the water." Unwatched in the confusion, the boy hurled the rotting carcass into the waves. The fish swam away, diving down and then arrowing up into the air to show its perfect gleaming flank in the last rays of twilight.

Covenant looked up to ensure that Seareaper had seen the splash and what followed after. Then the beggar stepped onto

the dock and tugged the rope away from the post on the pier.

Seareaper let the foaming water nudge the *Childsbreath* away from the dock toward her anchor in deeper water. On the pier, the disappointment of the remaining villagers turned to anger. They sought the beggar, but he was not there. No one seemed to know where he had gone.

THREE

The Face
Between the
Pages

W HERE IS COVENANT?" ASKED BEAUTY.

"Where he has chosen to be," answered Wordsmith. "Come and see, if you wish." He drew her to the west-facing window of his tower, and they watched as the view steadily magnified itself, over and over again, to show the figure of the beggar walking along a lonely seashore.

"In all this land," said Wordsmith, "I have seen no corner that is not his."

"But not all hearts are his."

"No, but remember that I can see only places here, and things, and not into houses or hearts." He gestured to the fifth window. "Only there may I see things that are not to be seen otherwise, and I see through that window but do not control what it shows."

"Or always understand it," she added softly, moving her hands along his arm and kneading his shoulder. He bent his back to her ministrations and cradled his head on the table, nudging the litter of papers and leather to one side.

"I have been watching him," murmured Wordsmith from between his hands.

"What is he doing?" asked Beauty.

"I am not sure," shrugged Wordsmith. "I can see many miles from this window, but sound does not carry here. Death is there, and now sadness and anger. I will not know the full story until I meet him again. When he has finished in this village, I am to leave here and find him along the road to another place."

"So many things you have seen figured. Are all of those people coming here? Who will be next?" she wondered. "They continue to come even when he is not here."

"It will not be long. Covenant said before he left that our company would grow before he returned."

The shadows fell along the seashore, and they could see no more from the window. Only the strange fifth window continued to swirl and bloom and reveal marvels to the man appointed to see its secrets.

*   *   *

Beauty descended and found the Chameleon Lady in one of the lower rooms.

"Are you in need of anything I can bring you?" Beauty asked.

The face before her blurred before settling into yet another countenance. "No, there is nothing you have the power to bring me. If there were, I'm convinced you would have by now." She looked up and smiled. "You have been most kind to me. You treat me as though I am still the same person you saw yesterday."

"Aren't you?"

"Not to your eyes."

Beauty shrugged. "I try to look for the person beneath the face anyway. It is not impossible with you, just harder."

"You have given to me freely and have asked nothing of me. Why?"

"I spoke those same words when first I came here," Beauty said. "We can give kindness and mercy only because we have received the same here ourselves—from Covenant."

"Tell me more of Covenant and this house."

"I have been here only a handful of months, and yet there is so much to say that I do not know where to begin."

"Start with yourself, if you please. Why are you here? You are beautiful enough to be celebrated in Glory."

"I was," said Beauty softly, "but Glory turned its back on me, and I turned my back on Glory. On a road into the wilderness I came upon a beggar and a handsome man, sitting on a rock and awaiting my footsteps. Each one gave me a road to choose with promises at the end. Even though Fame was attractive, I did not trust him. He offered me more of the same life I had tasted in Glory and had grown weary of."

A troubled look spread over the lady's changing eyes. "I have heard of Fame, but I have never seen him."

"I have seen him several times since that day . . . It is often hard to remember that though he is handsome and tall and powerful, his image is a mask. He means evil to anyone who seeks Covenant."

"Why should he hate Covenant?"

"I do not know the details," Beauty admitted, "but they have long been foes. Theirs is an ancient feud, going deeper than the bone."

The Chameleon Lady's next question was followed by another answer that raised more questions, and they talked long over the glowing fire.

* * *

Far from Glory, and far from Graycove, another fire burned late in a dwelling in one of the smaller villages. There, wrapped in his own solitude, a young man turned the pages of the ancient book again and wondered when its prophecies would come true.

" 'The greatest warrior of all will come,' " he murmured, remembering and only half seeing the words.

It is time, he thought, *to see if these promises have come true. Someone in Glory must know the truth behind the rumors of the man who sells written wisdom in the marketplace and invokes the name of the Elder God. I must go and see if he is the one.*

" 'When the hour of need is greatest,' " he recited aloud to no one but himself and the shadows, " 'the great warrior will appear, though only one will know him when he comes . . .

" 'And he will wield the sword of justice and the blade of righteousness,' like *this* . . ." He gestured in the darkness and prayed that he would live to see this warrior.

The shadows fell thickly from his thin body, and for a moment the shape of a giant danced upon the wall.

Then he sank back into himself, banked the fire and slept. In the morning he put on his cloak and wrapped his book in a leather pouch. Then he went out into the light and began the day's walk to Glory, seeking the man in the marketplace who stood and sold his curious books.

He found Wordsmith there on one of the street corners, gazing at the crowds but not seeing them. The expression in his eyes hinted that he watched the dance of distant planets rather than the parade of people.

The young man peered closely into Wordsmith's face. "You are not the one," he said disappointedly.

"I am Wordsmith," he answered. "Who are you looking for?"

"I am looking for the light of an old promise. I am looking for the mighty warrior who is to come."

"I am not a mighty warrior; I am a hobbling scribbler who dreams dreams and sells the words in the market."

The young man's face lost its disappointed look. "Do you sell wisdom, then?" he asked.

Wordsmith regarded him with open curiosity. "I sell the wisdom of the Elder God," he answered. "These books hold my words, but it is not my wisdom."

"I believe," said the young man, "that you may know the man I have been seeking." His eyes gleamed with a fierce and sudden light, and Wordsmith knew that he had seen this face in the visions of the fifth window. "You must tell me the secret of an old prophecy."

"What secrets I know, I share gladly," said Wordsmith. "But there are countless things I do not understand, and prophecies are the deepest of mysteries."

"Yet they are true."

"If real prophecies, then very true indeed. But they remain dense and dark, and often not understood until after they have come to be."

"I have here an old book," said the young man. "I would ask you a question about it."

Wordsmith examined the book, probing the pages with his fingers. "I know nothing of this book," concluded Wordsmith, "save that it is very old and that the script is tiny and hard to read."

"I can read it well; I know it by heart."

"Tell me the story," asked Wordsmith. "Perhaps I have seen this book in a dream, but I do not know what is in it. Is there a sword? And a warrior?"

"Then you do know of the book!"

"No, but I am shown many things that I do not understand until they happen. Come, the day is almost done and there are few buyers here, so let us pack these books away and go to the House of Covenant. We may talk there and have no interruption."

"The House of Covenant?"

"Covenant is the reason I am here. He is not in the City just now, but when he returns, he can answer your questions. His answers, however, may give you new questions. Every word he says is true, but not every word is clear at the time it is spoken. He seems to know all and see all, but he tells only when it is time."

* * *

The two men sat in one of the small rooms in the house in Glory. The remains of a meal littered the table between them.

"I have had this book for many years," the stranger said, "and my fingers have almost worn their way through the pages. This book has been my secret because I have heard few mention the name of the Elder God. But that name I have heard from your lips, and I was told it is here in your books.

"When I look at the book long enough," he went on, "and gaze at the words, and try to peer behind them, I can begin to see a face appearing between the pages."

"A face? Whose face?"

"I wish I knew him. It is the Warrior of the Elder God, Dreadnought the Freeblade, the mighty fighter who will come. I believe that I will see his face before I die, and if I can find him, I will offer him my service."

"The Warrior of the Elder God?" asked Wordsmith. "I know of the Elder God, but not this Warrior."

"The High Warrior, one who will be an earthly fighter on behalf of the Elder God, a mighty man who will walk with him, talk with him, obey him and be a sword of justice for him," recited the young man.

"And it is this face you are looking for?"

"Yes."

"You were disappointed when you saw me. You had heard of me, and you hoped to find that face upon my head?"

"Yes."

Wordsmith shook his head sadly. "I am sorry to have disappointed you. However, there is another here who knows much of old books," he continued. "Let us seek his counsel as well."

Wordsmith left, sought Binder and returned with him.

Binder lovingly perused the pages, well-worn by gentle handling and incessant turning of the vellum sheets. "It is not a book I have seen before," he said, "nor am I familiar with this sort of binding. It is old—very old. How long have you had it?"

"Two dozen years. It was given to me at my birth by an ancient woman who lived in the village."

"And there was no message left with it? No prophecy?"

"The book itself is the prophecy, and the message. I have read it, and I believe it with all my heart, and I almost understand it."

"Read it to both of us," urged Wordsmith, "that we might hear it and tell you what we know."

He laughed. "I need not *read* it! I know every word by heart."

He recited the full story, and after that they were silenced by wonder.

"The one who should answer you is not here," Wordsmith finally said, "but you are welcome to wait here until he returns. Tell us your name, that we may tell Covenant who waits for him."

The young man looked away from the flickering candle into the dancing darkness. "I am called Fearshadow," he said in a low voice, "but I despise that name."

"Then your name lies dead behind you at the door, if you wish it," said Wordsmith. "The master of this house gives good names to all who come here, and old names are quickly forgotten."

"But why not keep my name?" asked Fearshadow bitterly. "I have lived down to its meaning all my life, trembling at every hint of darkness, shunning all possible pain . . . I am not a brave man. Perhaps that is why I seek the company of the brave."

Wordsmith lifted his hand in surrender. "As you wish. I have no authority in this house to take names away or give new ones. Covenant will have the final word with you when he returns."

"And how long will that be?" asked Binder.

"I do not know," answered Wordsmith. "He is a long way from Glory, and I leave tomorrow to meet him in the wilderness."

"May I go with you?" asked Fearshadow eagerly. "I would see if *he* is the one."

"No," replied Wordsmith. "He has bid only me to come to him. I know where I will meet him, but I do not know what we are to do or where we will go from there or when we will return."

"He has not told you these things?"

Wordsmith eyed the young man for a moment. "He has not revealed all his thoughts to us, but he has revealed to us himself and his power as well. And to know him is to trust him and to follow at his command."

Fearshadow failed to find a reply.

"Think of this, Fearshadow," continued Wordsmith. "You have sworn allegiance to this warrior, even though you do not know if he is alive or even real. I have pledged my loyalty to Covenant, because of all men he is most real, and his call is to be trusted."

"But I would see if this Covenant is Dreadnought the Freeblade himself. How could it be otherwise? Look at his power and at the words of the prophecy."

"Covenant may or may not be the Freeblade. He has many names, but that is not one he has revealed to us. He already carries the words and the grace of the Elder God, but I cannot envision him with a sword in his hand.

"The hardest duty for the faithful is to wait patiently. I saw your book and your face in my dreams, and nothing is shown to me there in vain. Wait here, and learn the ways of this house. We shall return, and then you shall have your answer."

FOUR

The Boy from the Sea

A LATE FIRE BURNED IN SEAREAPER'S COTTAGE. THE FISHER-man sat crumpled in a wooden chair, watching the flames devour the splintered wood. Covenant leaned against the doorjamb, half-concealed from the flickering light. He could see Wavewatcher standing useless vigil in one darkened room behind.

"You charmed the fish we caught," said the wrinkled, leath-ery fisherman.

"I did," said the beggar.

"And you doubled the weight of my coppers."

"I did."

"And you made magic with the fish that perished long ago."

"That too."

"You offered me my son, but you have not given him."

"I have been waiting for you to challenge my words."

"Why are you still here? I am not poor any longer. You saw to that."

"Not poor in pocket, at least. But you are still poor in other things."

"You speak riddles. If it were not for what you have done already, I would wish you to go straight away."

"I know that too. That is why I multiplied your fish, so that you would talk to me now. You are a hard man, believing only what you have seen and examined and held in your hand. I bring you knowledge of a different sort, as well as a challenge to believe that which you have not yet seen."

"Who are you?" Seareaper asked solemnly. "You have told me your name, but not who you are. I would not choose to have one such as you angry with me."

"You have earned only my disappointment, not my anger. That could come another day. You have done some tasks at my bidding, but you will not believe until you have seen. Now, have you not seen four miracles in a single day?" inquired Covenant. "Surely if I can turn fish long rotted into fresh, I can bring new life to a boy not yet buried."

Hope and sorrow fought behind Seareaper's eyes. "No one comes back from the dead," he spat, leaving his words in the air like a dare.

"No boat the size of yours can fill four wagons, but yours did," countered Covenant. "And no fish was ever spawned that spewed coppers from its mouth, yet you held one in your hand. And can you explain coppers that multiply themselves in your hand?"

"I had heard of such things before—empty tales. I did not believe the ancient stories."

"Why? Because they were ancient or because they were stories? Haven't you had your measure of miracles? What more do you want?"

The woman spoke for the first time, her voice flat as she

drifted in from the next room. "Today has been a day of nightmares," she said, "and the only cure for nightmares lies in our wildest dreams."

"And what is your wildest dream?" returned Covenant. "There are as many dreams as there are dreamers."

"We both want what we dare not ask for," she retorted, moving out of the darkness into the firelight. "How could our need be plainer to you?"

"Those fish were despised, worth nothing to you, to the others, even to the birds," said Covenant. "Yet I found it worthwhile to give them life anew. Is the boy of your heart worth less than a poison fish that no man will ever see again?" He did not expect a spoken answer, and received none. "Do you believe?" he continued.

"I begin to believe," said Seareaper slowly, "but I do not understand at all."

"Belief and wisdom are not the same thing. Behold!" He pointed through the inner door.

Behind them, the boy came sleepy from the shadows.

"He will be hungry," said Covenant. "He has not eaten for a long time."

*   *   *

He ate in contented silence. The boy watched his father, and his eyes were full of questions. The father watched the beggar, and his eyes were full of gratitude. The mother's eyes were full of her son, and Covenant watched them all.

Not until they had finished did anyone speak again. "You have given us much," said Seareaper, "yet you have asked for nothing." He offered his words as a statement, but the wonder in his voice was not veiled.

"I claim your boat—not now, but for a later service."

"The boat is yours."

"Keep her for me."

"The boat is yours," repeated the old fisherman. "I keep my promises too."

"I give her back to you again. Use her well. Someday I shall return for her. That again is my word. And when I return, perhaps your son will journey with me. He, too, may see some wondrous things."

"Wondrous things, indeed. The village will not soon forget this night, for all saw Foamrider lifeless on the sand, and all will see him alive again tomorrow."

"They did and they shall. But I say that you should call him Foamrider no longer; let Seaswallower be his name. That would do nicely for a boy who has inhaled the ocean and yet lives to sail upon it."

"New names come hard to the tongue."

"Nevertheless, it pleases me to bestow new names on those who encounter me. Names mark both power and privilege. And there are better names for you as well, if you will receive them."

"You have earned that right," the fisherman admitted. "Name us as you will."

"What should I rename you?" mused Covenant, while they awaited his decision. "I shall call you Deedtester, for you have tried my works and found them true." He turned to Wavewatcher. "And you shall be Joykeeper. I have overcome your ancient enemy for you, and never more shall you despise and fear the sea."

"Will you tell me again why must you give us new names?" she asked.

"There are reasons beyond your imagining," said Covenant. "Everyone has a name, at least one name. And one name will be better and more suited than the rest. Your first names were only guesses and high hopes, or darkness seen and curses. Now your names tell what you do. When the time is at hand, I shall give you the names you have possessed all along and never heard spoken. Your hearts will leap when I name your true names, and no earthly title will ever satisfy you again.

"Your final names shall say for all to see who you shall be

then. Some names will be given in shame, for shame, and worn for shame forever. Blessed are you who are named with good names. Twice blessed are you who are renamed for the tasks you are called to do. Thrice blessed are they who are renamed a final time forever, by the mouth of the one whose hands made them."

In the awed silence the man finally spoke. "Then only my boat has its old name. Unless you would rechristen her as well."

"No," said Covenant, as his face showed the presence of warm memories, "I named her already in the dream I sent you. Let it remain the *Childsbreath*. There is both irony and prophecy in it."

After their meal, Covenant led the three others down to the pier. Deedtester strode beside the beggar, while mother and child followed together behind them.

"Tell me," Deedtester called to Covenant, "would he have drowned today if you had come yesterday?"

"No. That is why I did not come yesterday. Would you have believed in anything less than death undone?"

Again the fisherman let his silence answer for him.

They reached the weathered wooden structure creaking out over the water, scoured of coppers now but still strewn with the stinking remains of old catches. "This pier needs cleansing," Covenant said. "Let us try our hand as the boy did." He threw a dead and blackened fish into the lively yet blacker water. They heard it splash away and saw the phosphorescent trail blooming behind it as it headed for open water.

The boy began to gather the rest of the discarded fish, his excitement increasing as one by one they splashed, flashed and headed out to sea. The others helped, but the splendid sight was the boy dancing in the waves, a silhouette against the reflected moonlight.

His parents stood together in the darkness, holding hands

and marveling. When they turned to face the land again, Covenant was gone.

*   *   *

"We did not thank him enough," said Deedtester to his wife later, as they sat at each other's side and watched wild images dance in the fire.

"Perhaps we shall try when he comes again," she replied, "*if* there is a next time."

"He has promised a next time," her husband said as they stared into the waning fire, "and he seems to keep his promises. We have not seen the last of him."

FIVE

Words
in the
Wilderness

WORDSMITH HELD BEAUTY'S HAND ACROSS THE TABLE. "Covenant has called me to go on a journey with him," he said quietly. "He has said that he has much for my eyes and ears alone."

"Will you be gone long?" she asked, tightening her fingers about his.

"I don't know," he replied, "but whether a long journey or a short one I must go."

"I wish you could stay here, or perhaps take me with you."

"So do I," he answered. "You were my free choice," continued Wordsmith in a voice almost too soft to be heard, "and I would ever choose that choice again. But Covenant calls, and it is a call that must be answered."

She nodded, and a tear spilled down her cheek.

"Are you afraid that you won't see me again?" he asked.

She nodded again, and the twin of the first tear marked her other cheek.

"Then fear not, because Covenant has said that our work here is not finished. And when has Covenant's word ever failed to come true?"

* * *

Covenant and Wordsmith met in the high desert, and their friendship was rekindled.

"I asked you to meet me on the way," said Covenant, "that I might talk to you and to you alone."

"And you have two fresh puzzles awaiting you in Glory," Wordsmith said. He went on to describe the Chameleon Lady and Fearshadow and their quests.

"They will have their answers," the beggar said, "when they have learned to ask the right questions."

"And you will give them new names as well, I assume."

"Yes."

"Are Fearshadow's words true?" Wordsmith asked. "It is a most amazing story."

"You have walked with me, and you know some of my ways. Do you think his story is true?"

"I do not know," admitted Wordsmith. "It tastes of the Elder God, but it deals with events I cannot imagine. Why should we need a swordsman? We are in peace here, not peril. And where should we find this swordsman?"

"He will find us. Do you doubt my word?"

"I do not doubt your sayings and your promises. I simply do not understand them."

"Be content in your ignorance for now," Covenant said, "for when the veil of darkness is finally lifted, you will have much sorrow before you find your joy again. And that, my friend, is why you should carry this book always." Covenant handed him a tiny leather-bound book.

Wordsmith took the gift with pleasure and carefully turned

the bright, translucent pages. "There is nothing in it," he said. "The pages are blank."

"That is because you have not filled it with words," Covenant replied.

"What words?"

"The words I have not yet spoken to you," he answered. "I must tell you many things—more than stories, more than legends, more than wishful thinking. What I tell you now, you will not understand—but you will record it anyway, and when the time has come, you will turn to it again."

"Is this why you bid me come with quill and ink, but no paper?"

Covenant nodded, and waved his hand for Wordsmith to be seated on a rock. Then Covenant spoke, a timeless stream of words about righteousness, and long-dormant evil now approaching, and war, and Fame, and enemies pressing in on every side. And what Wordsmith heard he wrote down, and it filled him with both sadness and hope.

The hours passed as they worked, one speaking with solemn gentleness and the other writing as fast as he could. When the words were done and the book was filled, Wordsmith laid his head on his folded hands and said, "These are great and mighty and fearful words indeed—but I can scarcely remember a word now."

"You do not need to remember," Covenant replied. "The book will make sense to you only when it is time."

In the morning they began to walk back to Glory.

* * *

"Covenant," asked Wordsmith, "was this land always like this?" He gestured at the arid spaces and sterile soil and forbidding mountain ranges about them.

"No," said Covenant. "It has decayed to this. It was once magnificent, and unspoiled."

"It is still magnificent, even in desolation."

"Some things cannot be destroyed. The earth shudders, and

buildings fall. Rivers carve new courses, and old coasts are exchanged for new beaches sanded from the heart of the sea. This is a restless earth."

"This is a beautiful land," Wordsmith said, "even though it is stark and brutal."

"Someday it shall be even more beautiful again, for it shall cease to be merely stark. This land was created for peace and happiness, which cannot dwell undimmed in the midst of darkness, despair and death. The land crumbles where Fame rules."

"Again, I do not understand. Does Fame rule, or does the King, or is it you who rules in secret?"

"Yes," Covenant answered simply. "The King holds the reins of power, but Fame's hands guide the hands that hold the reins. The King is only a royal shadow, a puppet, a toy, a mask. But someday the King must fall ill and die, and who will rule in his place? He has no children, no heritage, no prince or favored counselor waiting patiently in the treacherous darkness behind the throne."

"Is Fame his true name?"

"Recall that his other name is *Twister*."

"Is that his true name, or one you have given him?"

"His first name shimmered and scattered light; then he chose Fame for himself, and was branded Twister by the Elder God."

"And does he have a secret and final name?" Wordsmith asked.

"He does—and it will be terrible to hear. He will have no joy when the words are uttered."

SIX

Rockhaven

COVENANT AND WORDSMITH STOPPED IN THE DUST OF THE thin road and gazed down into the valley that opened itself before them.

"What was this place?" asked Wordsmith, pointing at the rubbled rock ruins ahead. "Was it once a village? There is fear here now. I can almost taste it."

"I know," said Covenant. "That is why we have come."

They walked down into silence and stone disarray.

"Someone lives here," said Wordsmith, "but where? There is scarcely any shelter left."

A man and his child emerged from the rocks to meet the travelers. The man held a bow with an arrow already nocked; like his father, the tiny boy held a toy bow and arrow.

"I thought you were the wolves again," muttered the man.

"There are human wolves as well," said the beggar, "but we are not wolves of either kind."

"Where are the walls?" asked Wordsmith. "You should not have to worry about a handful of wolves."

"Once there was a village here, with houses, stables, a stout wall. There was shelter here," said the man, "shelter and enough—until the ground shook and the walls crumbled and most died beneath the stones. Those who survived left, except for us."

"And you stayed here alone?" inquired Wordsmith.

"The ground in this valley is fertile," the man said. "The weather is warm, and there is water in abundance. Why should I leave?"

"Yet you live in fear of the wolves."

"Could you ignore them if your protection had crumbled?"

Covenant did not reply, but only gazed at the fallen walls.

The man walked about uneasily. Where he strode, the child strode; where he stopped, the child stopped.

"There is more damage here than was done by an earthquake," said Covenant. "Many of these stones have been rolled away from the places where they fell."

The man nodded, but said nothing.

"Who moved these stones away?" asked Covenant.

"I did," the man reluctantly acknowledged.

"Where are they now?"

"Down there," he pointed. "They line my garden and give us shade where the pool comes down from the mountains. I could move the stones down the hill to build new buildings," said the man defensively, "but not up the hill to rebuild the old ones. Not by myself. You cannot defend a wall that has fallen."

"No, you cannot. Even less can you defend a wall which has been carried away."

An uncomfortable silence enveloped them before the man grudgingly asked if they needed water or a place to rest their feet.

Covenant accepted for them, and they ascended to a cleft in the rocks, a broad cave defended by only a few roughly placed boulders. Smaller stones and mortar had been pounded into the gaps; even so, it was barely worth the name of shelter. The cave was wide but shallow, with little protected room for a fire. A woman was struggling to create a flame in the broken oven, muttering over the crumbly bark and green wood. She looked up briefly and angrily, then turned again to the unborn fire. The spark from her stones was feeble, and Wordsmith did not think any fire would endure even a light rain.

Covenant looked sadly at their poor quarters.

"The wolves come every night," the man explained. "There is no other place to hide."

"If the walls were repaired, you would have no reason to huddle in the cave."

"If the walls were repaired," said the man sharply, "many of my problems would be solved."

"You have the child here," said Covenant. "Let him defend the walls."

"But he is only a babe!" snorted the man. "It is *I* who must protect *him!*"

"Against certain dangers, perhaps," answered Covenant. "There are some perils that perhaps only a child could discern, and some burdens that only a child could carry."

The man would not look at them now, but spat into a brittle shrub and began to shape the sand aimlessly with his foot.

The child, doing as his father did, spat dryly at the bush and drew figures in the dust.

"I have come," announced Covenant, "that you might rebuild these walls. If you wish to survive the wilderness this valley has become, you must undo the damage that has been done here—both by nature and by your own hands."

"Who are you?" the man asked bluntly.

"I am Covenant," said the beggar. "This is Wordsmith, my friend and companion."

"I am Audin," said the man dully. "This is my child, Carlin, and there is my wife, Sabrin. Where do you come from?"

"There is a time for questions," Covenant said, "and there is a time for obedience. You must carry the first rock now. The rest may come later. Take the one that lies at your feet and lift it." He smiled. "It is more important than you can possibly imagine."

Reluctantly, Audin picked up a boulder and lugged it up the hill to the old wall. He thunked it into its former place and picked his way down the hill again, breathing hard.

"Now what?" he asked the beggar arrogantly. "Will the wolves be afraid of that?"

"Watch and see," said Covenant quietly. "You have done well. Rest for a moment, and have your eyes opened."

The child—doing as his father had done—selected a small rock at his feet, hefted it in his fists, carried it up the hill and laid it carefully on the remains of the wall.

"And again," said Covenant to Audin. "Grasp the largest stone you can lift and replace it."

He did so with enormous difficulty, and afterward sat panting on the ground near Covenant.

They watched as the child grasped a hewn boulder three times his own size and lifted it into the air.

Audin began to leap to his aid, but Covenant restrained him with one arm. "Say nothing to him," he commanded. "He does not know this is beyond his power. He does not know which work is impossible and which is merely difficult," said Covenant. "He is only doing what he has seen you do already."

The stone rolled into its rightful place.

"I do not believe what I am seeing!" breathed the man.

"You shall come to believe many things more difficult than this. For the childlike, nothing shall be impossible. Do likewise."

Audin bent to the stones before him and found them as light as the boy believed. Dizzy, he could not restrain a chuckle of relief in the face of wonder and power.

"If the two of you work diligently," said Covenant, "the stones will not weary you, and you may finish before dark. It would be a pleasant surprise against the wolves.

"Do not forget me," added the beggar, "or my friend here. We shall meet again. You live in isolation here, but I reassure you that your hopes still lie in Glory."

"Don't go!" said Audin. "I want to know what your power is."

"You will learn more of me in times to come. For now, behold what has happened, and accept my new names for the two of you: you are Stonesetter in my eyes, and the boy shall be called Featherstone."

Stonesetter's eyes accepted the command, though he did not understand. Covenant offered only his infectious smile for an explanation. With a warm wave he drifted across the hill through the passage to the open kitchen. There he bent to help Sabrin, still focused upon the stubborn fire. But she urged him away, saying roughly, "It may be a poor place, but it is my place, and I have always managed. You've taken up my man's time already, and I won't give you any of mine."

Covenant's offered assistance blunted itself on her suspicion and disbelief. He smiled sadly and let the rotten tinder crumble in her fingers. He abandoned her territory to her again and went outside to see a man at work and a child at play, and both rebuilding the wall.

"Doubt can be challenged and cured," he said to Wordsmith, "but there is no remedy for stubborn disbelief. The walls here are not the only things made of stone."

SEVEN

A Cure
for
Chameleon

WHEN COVENANT AND WORDSMITH RETURNED TO GLORY, Fearshadow was waiting for them on the stone steps of the house. He bounded down to the street to meet them, peering anxiously into Covenant's face; once again, he was disappointed.

"Do not be sad," Covenant said. "I know your quest, and I promise you that your heart's desire will not remain unfulfilled."

"When? How? Who?" he asked impatiently.

"Let us eat," said Covenant, drawing him along to the house. "Let us have our leisure with the others, and then we will talk. Beauty has prior claim upon Wordsmith, and you are not the only one who has come searching for an answer: there is a lady as well."

"Yes," he said, feeling suddenly ashamed of his eagerness, "she is inside. I hope that you can help her."

Their meal was happy and noisy, and the Chameleon Lady sat patiently observing, laughing here and there, until all were finished and only she and Covenant sat in the room.

"I have heard many good things about you," she began.

"All of them are true," he replied, his smile carrying away any offense that the words might have caused.

His candor surprised her; she hesitated, then spoke directly to her need. "Wordsmith has told you of me?" she asked.

"Yes, and I know more than he has told me."

"How many people have you seen in my face tonight?" she asked bluntly.

"Only one," Covenant said.

"Then you are not affected by the magic?"

"No."

"Beauty said as much. Is it, indeed, a true face, or does it shift from one image to another?"

"The face I see is the true one, but it is not the face you bear here."

"Is it a good face?"

"It is a very fine face, but it is hidden. You have been false," he continued gently, "and for now you must bear the burden of falsehood."

She fingered her necklace. "I have tested the metal," she said. "It will bend but will not break, and no tool can cut it. It shines like gold, but is more resistant than diamond."

She looked up. "Will not *your* magic melt it?" she asked hopefully.

Covenant traced his finger along the line of the necklace and shook his head. "Some magic is best cured by magic," he said, "and some magic is best remedied a better way. The highest kind of magic is neither angry nor violent," he continued, "nor does it have destruction as its purpose."

"Is there a way to unwind this chameleon curse?"

"There is, but it is not simple, and it is not easy to find. What has been cursed by a man must be cured by a man. If there is a powerful man who will place his pledge around this one and make you his own, he will end the curse. But even then he will not know what you truly look like until after the first night with you."

"Who would take such a chance as that?" she asked, expecting no answer and receiving none. She thought, and then said, "Will a man, indeed, solve my problems, or only cause more? Men have been the cause of my greatest griefs."

"Only he who has the power to bring you great grief can also bring you great joy. A man who cannot hurt you cannot heal you." He waved his hand in the air. "Nor is it written anywhere that you must find or even accept this cure. You are alive and well and need not have a man to be welcome and useful here. The flesh fades, and all faces change with time; you are not the only one who strives with a visage that is not the same from day to day.

"There is hope," he continued, "and there are promises, but now is not the time to talk of them. A better time will come later. Besides, I bring you not only a welcome but also a task for you, a task that no one else here can do."

Her eyes brightened. "What can I do that lies in my hands alone?" she wondered.

"You can deliver a special message to the King," answered Covenant evenly.

"The King!" she exclaimed. "No one goes there without invitation!"

"Or those who have the proper face, and your face just now is in the eye of the beholder. To the guards at the gates, you will be one of the servants. To the servants inside, you will be another visitor not to be noticed. And to the King, you will be his Queen."

"But she has been dead for twenty years!" she objected.

"She lives in his heart still," observed Covenant, "and her

beauty will never fade for him.

"He has many advisors, but they are weak; he trusts none of them. He hears their words, and he nods, but then he does what is right in his own eyes. But he will fall before you and beseech you to speak. He will hear you because he believes he has already heard her voice from beyond the grave.

"I have removed all obstacles from your path, and nothing can prevent you now but your own fears."

She pondered the idea. "But if I go, what must I say to him?" she asked.

"When you are ready to leave for the palace, I will teach you what you should say. The King dreams much, and even a forgotten god can still speak in dreams." He smiled again, and they went on to talk of other things.

EIGHT

The Search for Freeblade

FEARSHADOW STOOD IN THE HIGH TOWER AND MARVELED at Wordsmith's windows.

"Are these things true already?" he asked.

"What you see in these four windows is happening as you see it," Wordsmith said. "As for the fifth window, I am never sure. Things that could happen, things that should happen, things that will happen . . . it is hard to tell the difference until the reality arrives."

"All I see are blurs and strange signs and uncountable stars."

"Few people see things clearly there."

"And you are one of the special people?"

Wordsmith hesitated. "I would not call myself special—rather would I call this a very special window."

"And you see visions in its depths?"

"I do."

Fearshadow nodded. "I think I understand. I see a single vision, and that within the pages of my book."

"Does anyone else see that same vision there?"

"No."

"Then you understand perfectly."

They looked down at the street and saw Candle heading toward his shop.

"Is it Candle who supports this house?" Fearshadow asked.

"Some of his profits are used here, but this house does not depend on him or his work," replied Wordsmith. "He is a trader in fine goods, and he meets many who come to Glory for the first time and do not know where to begin to see what is here.

"Some find more than they expected," he added. "I have put all their stories in this book—at least, as far as their stories go. The endings are still unknown, though Covenant has given us many bright promises." He waved the stranger to a seat while opening his book. "Candle and Moonflower, first united in life and then in death, and now reunited in life again." He turned the pages. "Trueteller, the mother of Moonflower. Once an outcast and now a matron of much honor. Lionheart, a shaggy-headed young man with a harvest of infants and ancients abandoned as useless and unwanted in the wilderness, a man who rides lions through the darkness and roars with them in their wild and exuberant power." He smiled inside at the image and went on. "Binder, once a narrow-visioned collector of fine books, now a man who has found more value in the souls of humanity and in books than in their outward bindings. And Firecolt and Flamerider—the fire brothers—the two street boys Binder rescued from the flames that consumed his house after an earthquake.

"And there was Woebearer, the hunchback, who emerged from a mysterious and shameful life to spend the rest of his days absorbing other people's pains and carrying other people's burdens. Woebearer went ahead to the City when all the wax of the candle of his body had been consumed."

He gestured to the back of the house below them. "There are favored beasts as well, asleep in the stables at the back: Roadreeler the horse, who carried Trueteller and Candle and Moonflower to Glory, and Kingsburro the donkey, who served first Trueteller and then Covenant.

"All of these—men, women, children and animals—are the Company of Covenant. Covenant, the beggar who walks like a king and who comes in the name of the Elder God. All have been given new lives and new hearts by Covenant; most have been given new names as well."

"Covenant," said Fearshadow. "Why has he not spoken to me yet? He knows of my search, and he said only that we would talk of it later. Since that day I have scarcely seen him across the room."

"He has his own times and his own ways. I do not pretend to understand them, but I do value the gifts that he eventually brings our way.

"Bide your time—it is his time, too, and he seems to have an abundance of it."

* * *

The next day Fearshadow found Covenant sitting alone before breakfast.

"The one you seek is here in Glory," said Covenant without preamble.

The words burned in Fearshadow's heart like a welcome flame. "He is here? Where? Shall I see him?"

"You shall see him."

"May I serve him?"

"Not as you thought to serve, but you shall do his bidding. Go and search," Covenant said. "He is not to be found in the way you believe."

"Will I know him when I see him?"

"You will know his face," Covenant promised, "though you

will scarcely believe your own eyes. You must search diligently or you will not find his face."

Fearshadow was gone without another word. Late that night, and on each of the four succeeding nights, he returned in disappointment, turning to his book again by candlelight, seeking to refresh his memory of the face between the pages.

"I have disturbed everyone," he said to Covenant at last. "I have peered into every face in Glory and not found him. I have done all and found nothing."

"You have not yet peered into *every* face in Glory," said Covenant. "Perhaps you are looking too hard, and in all the difficult places.

"How long has it been since you beheld your own face?" asked Covenant.

"What do I care for *my* face?" responded Fearshadow, gesturing at his book. "I have been searching other faces to see *this* one."

"Look into the book again," Covenant commanded, "and tell me of the face you see there."

Fearshadow gazed into the pages and was silent for a while. "I see him again now," he said at last, "and clearly. He is not tall, or broad, but his eyes burn with holy fire, and he wields an unnatural strength that he does not claim as his own. His face glows with his calling, and foes quake at the sight. He is a bloody man and bowed with pain, but not defeated."

"What is a book?" asked Covenant.

Fearshadow, bewildered, spoke slowly. "A book is a group of pages bound together," he said. "There are words written on the pages, and the words make a story."

"A book can be much more than that," suggested Covenant. "You understand only the half because you see only the half: this is not only a book," he stressed, "but a mirror."

Fearshadow stared at him without comprehension. "A book reflects nothing save the spirit and intent of its author."

"It does reflect that, and more than you might think." He

took Fearshadow's arm and led him down the long halls to Covenant's mirror.

"Look into the mirror," suggested Covenant.

Fearshadow did so, and what he saw there staggered him.

He finally turned to Covenant. "Can it be?" he asked.

"It can," answered Covenant. "It can, and it is. *There* is the face you have been seeking. The words have soaked into your heart as well as your imagination, and shaped your face as well as your soul. That which you have yearned to find you have become.

"You have searched long for him; he was with you every step on every road, and yet you continually looked away. It was fitting that you did so, for you have learned to seek the best in others first. In futility you learned patience, and in meditation you have absorbed a noble countenance."

Covenant reached above the mirror, where a fine wooden sword was carved deep into the grain of the frame. He grasped it, and it came alive in his hands, a right blade, deadly, keen and sharp, a weapon that glittered even in the twilight of the hall and further heightened Fearshadow's awe.

"Kneel before me," commanded Covenant. The young man obeyed without question. "I know your old name," continued Covenant, "but now it is dead, as your old self is dead. Receive, then, this double name of honor. I name you Dreadnought Freeblade—Swordsman of the Elder God, Champion of the Company of Covenant and Defender of the Child."

He glided the gleaming flat of the blade over Freeblade's cheeks, and then commanded him to rise and take the sword.

"This is now your companion and your charge," Covenant said sadly. "I wish that you would never have need to pull it from its sheath, but you shall be forced to draw much blood with it."

Freeblade's tears dropped freely to the floor, but none of them were wasted.

"Has there ever been such a blade as this?" he breathed.

"No," Covenant said simply. "There has not and will never be."

"Is it enchanted?"

"It is holy—that is better yet. Worthy kings carried it, for it was set apart in honor, and it in turn was honored by them. Not all the kings were selfish, evil or withdrawn, and not all of the king's men were more interested in their own comfort than in the prosperity of the land and its people."

Freeblade looked up from the blade at last and met Covenant's gaze. "What must I do now?" he asked.

"No battles, for now. Read your book again, knowing this time that the warrior is you."

"Covenant," he said, "who wrote this book?"

"There were other dreamers before Wordsmith, faithful men and women long since dead. The woman who wrote this book had scarcely left her childhood behind when she filled these pages. She was mother five times past to the elderly woman who left it you as a legacy."

NINE

A
Measure
of Mercy

TRUETELLER CAME SEEKING COVENANT IN THE SILENCE OF the early morning.

"Do you believe in dreams?" she asked quietly.

"For some people I am only a dream," he replied. "Do you believe in me?"

"Yes. You know I do. I have more reason than any to know that you are real."

"Then you should believe in some dreams as well."

"Only the good ones?" she asked.

"No. Some good dreams will come true, but so will some nightmares."

"I'm not sure if this is a dream or a nightmare."

"Tell me, then, and we will see if it might hold a seed of truth."

She took a deep breath but found no easy way to begin. "He is alive, isn't he?" she finally burst forth. "I saw him again in my dreams. He is alive, and he is a captive."

"You have not asked these questions before," Covenant stated.

"No."

"But these dreams are not new."

"No. I have seen my husband many times in my dreams—often in chains, sometimes underground—but always alive, always in trouble and despair. I have had them for many years, but never so frequently as now, and never so vividly as last night."

Covenant smiled. "But you have never mentioned them to me."

"I thought them wishful thinking—a fantasy—a desperate hope."

"All hope is desperate when it is not yet fulfilled."

"But now I know that many true things happen before we are ready to see or accept them . . . and I hesitated to ask you, because you have done so much for me already."

"Is that not a good reason for asking further favors? One does not number gifts where love exists. All you need do is tell me what you would know of me."

She drew breath and exhaled slowly. "First, I would know if my dreams are true. Is he alive?"

"He is."

Her heart leaped; she squeezed her eyes shut and could not trust herself to breathe.

"Is he free to return to me?" she finally asked.

"No."

Again she held her thoughts for a span of heartbeats, choosing her words carefully, both wanting to know and not wanting to know the answer.

"Has he forgotten me?"

"He has never forgotten you. You are the strongest single

hope that keeps him alive."

She sat and wept for joy, and he did not bother her. When her tears slackened, she said, "I have never believed he was dead, even though he vanished nearly twenty years ago. *Can he be rescued?*"

"Not by any man—or any woman, for that matter."

"But you can."

"You cannot guess the source of his rescue," said Covenant, "but it may begin with the works of your own hands."

"I will do anything you ask."

"I ask that you trust and obey and give mercy while keeping silence. None of what you are told to do will make sense to you, and I will not explain it until all things are put right."

She nodded her agreement.

"Go out into the wilderness today," he said, "beyond the walls of Glory, and seek for a wounded animal that needs mercy. Then let your heart tell you what to do, even if you are afraid."

So she went out, images of a wounded rabbit or kit fox dancing in her head. She remembered fondly the many small wild animals that had ventured to her outcasts' cottage in older days.

But the sun reached its peak, and she found nothing.

The sun began its slide into the west, and she found nothing.

She was hot and hungry, weary of the search, but because of Covenant she kept on. What she did find left her breathless and very much afraid: a great eagle fluttered helplessly but angry on the ground, a long and wicked arrow lodged through the root of its wing. She gazed at the great bird for a moment, and it glared at her.

"Do not be afraid of me," she said suddenly. "I come from Covenant." *Do not be afraid of me?* she thought. *I am the one who is afraid. It could kill me with that beak and shred me with those claws.*

Its gleaming black feathers were matted thickly with recent

blood, and its eyes were glazed with pain.

She stepped forward, despite her doubts and in the face of her fears. The eagle drew itself up and hissed, but it did not give ground.

She began to repeat Covenant's name over and over, holding her hands out with open palms and advancing slowly.

Its good wing hammered the air vainly and it screeched at her, but it did not prevent her approach. She crept closer, afraid but still moving, until her shadow fell across the wounded bird.

Stretching out her hand, she hesitantly touched the arrow and shuddered as she felt the shaft grating against the bone. She drew back her hand, appalled.

"I cannot help you here," she whispered. "I shall have to carry you home."

She spoke to it soothingly for a long time, and at last she dared to touch it again. It consented to be caressed, and at long last was cradled and hoisted to her shoulder. It clung awkwardly and held its injured wing rigidly out over her head. Its talons pressed into her flesh, and she winced as a few trickles of blood began to inch down her arm.

But she moved on with both purpose and wonder, and the bird did not fight her.

Night fell before she returned to Glory, and no one saw her come through the gates with her peculiar burden. The dark feathers of the bird were only a smaller shadow in the vast shadow of the night.

Back at the house, Covenant's surprising hands snapped the ends from the arrow like straw, then deftly drew the shaft from the bird's flank. Trueteller washed the wound and packed it with spices and medicines.

"You might carry him to the roof," Covenant suggested. "He will find both comfort and privacy there, and no walls to close in his spirit."

"Will he fly away?"

"Not until he is ready."

On her way through the house she met Candle and some of the others.

"What is his name?" asked Candle, as they admired the great bird from a respectful distance.

"I do not know what his name is," she answered. "I did not know for certain it was a him. But Covenant knows such things, and he has not named him, so I shall call him Farsight."

"Why?"

"Because both Covenant and this bird see much farther than I can, and their ways are ever beyond me. And they are both part of a puzzle he has challenged me to untwist."

"A puzzle?"

But Trueteller would say no more. She gently carried the great bird to the roof and left the others standing below in the candlelit dark.

Once set down on the roof, Farsight tucked his head into the tangle of his wings and bandages and slept.

She lay down on the roof beside him and was soon asleep as well.

* * *

Farsight was already awake when Trueteller stirred in the light before the sunrise. He darted his head from side to side and hissed urgently at her, though without malice.

She decided he was hungry. At a loss over what to feed him, she returned with a basket of fruit and some bread. He tore at the bread, but was suspicious of the fruit until she sliced a piece and fed it to him. Then he hungrily gobbled the rest of that fruit, and more after.

Then she went to find Covenant. "And now?" she said to him. "I have done everything you asked of me."

"So now it is time to do something else. You must wait patiently until his wing heals."

"Covenant?" she asked as he turned away. "I have another question, but not about my husband."

"Speak it."

"Will I also have a grandchild of my own to hold someday? One child was a joy, but not enough."

"Some day," he answered, "and she will be a first to you and a first for many." He gently declined to explain further.

Later, she fed Farsight some strips of meat, and he ate, but was not satisfied until fruit was brought as well. He seemed particularly fond of cavada, soft purplish fruits that Candle often bought from a place many miles south of Glory, a remote valley village on the very edge of the kingdom.

"Eagles don't eat fruit," said Firecolt, who was standing near when she asked Candle for more cavada. Flamerider agreed.

"This one does," answered Trueteller simply.

— TEN —

Return
to the
Rock

LIONHEART WAS BUSY PLAYING WITH A CHILD IN THE NURS-
ery and did not see Covenant in the crowded room until he
spoke at the young man's elbow.

"Are you satisfied here?"

Lionheart nodded.

"Have not all my promises come true?" continued the beggar. "Did I not say that you would have children and parents
in abundance if you followed me?"

"Yes," said Lionheart, "all that and more." His eyes wan-
dered fondly around the room of infants and ancients, frequently coming to rest on his tiny niece, Woodswaif. "I have
rescued them all," he continued, "at your bidding and my
pleasure." His voice softened. "But there is still one who is not
here, and so you have one last promise to keep."

It was Covenant's turn to nod. "Tonight he will join you."

The words sunk in, and Lionheart reached for his cloak, a blanket and a pouch of food. "Then I should have left already!" he exclaimed. "The sun is almost gone, and there is not time to reach the rock even before the morning! I was a full day on that road with Woodswaif."

Covenant stretched out a hand and stopped his rush. "True. But tonight there will be no need to ride gently or timidly. You have ridden the beasts many times, but have you ever raced another rider?" His eyes twinkled as he held forth the challenge.

"I would, indeed, race," Lionheart answered gladly, "if it would not harm the lions."

"Harm the lions?" Covenant laughed. "To make them run and roam and roar? Why do you think they were made? It is in their nature to be bold and quick and tireless, and it is they who have been gentle with you."

The two men passed through the house, the streets of Glory and the great gates, putting a field between themselves and the stone walls. They stopped in the deeper dusk beneath the trees, and Covenant called to the darkness. Suddenly the lions were there, looming out of the uncertainties of the shadows—not just two or four, but a dozen or more.

"They have all come," said Covenant, "to see this ride." He beckoned the two largest lions to him. "Behold the champions of the prides! Choose your mount. I shall ride the other, and the rest shall follow."

Lionheart could see that many more lions had arrived, more than he could number in the shifting shadows. The prides gathered—restless, eager, ready. Some were old and lean and purposeful, while others were young and excited and unsure of the occasion, hardly able yet to avoid their own feet.

They chose and mounted. Lionheart twisted his fist tightly into the mane before him, and with a single shout from Covenant they were off—a launch of lions leaving a vast roar behind them in the night. The rush of blackness blew Lionheart's hair back, and he hunched down for safety and balance in the leaping madness. All were ready to run, but the two beasts beneath the men settled quietly to the fierce race. The others roared and called to one another, then slowly lapsed into a silence framed by the whorfs of their exhalations. He could not see where they were going, and his fear took time to fade, for this night he was not the master of the wild cats; he was not directing them, but being pulled along in their wake.

A river of great cats poured through the starlit land, ignoring the roads of man and needing none of their own. Their running was more serious now, silent and intense, less exuberant but every bit as joyful. Their feet pounded the earth, their breath exploded half-seen in the air, and their legs devoured the miles at a rate Lionheart could not guess.

There was no way to pace the passing of time, for even the stars blurred overhead in the swiftness of their flight. Lionheart soared unseated in the air as much as he clung with his knees; but even though the hills rose and fell beneath them and the way wavered from side to side, the ride was not rough despite its reckless majesty.

Lionheart drank in the power and the speed, and his heart was glad within him for more reasons than he could think to name.

At last the moon gave them a brief glimpse of their path, and Lionheart could see ahead a rank of trees he recognized. But any new thoughts were lost in the need to hang on as the two lions accelerated away in a final sprint. First one led and then the other, then neither could be said to be ahead or behind.

They plunged into the line of trees as one, branches crackling at their sides. Covenant cried "Well done!" and the lions sprawled heavily but happily in the clearing by the great rock.

The others, left behind in the final dash, spilled into the

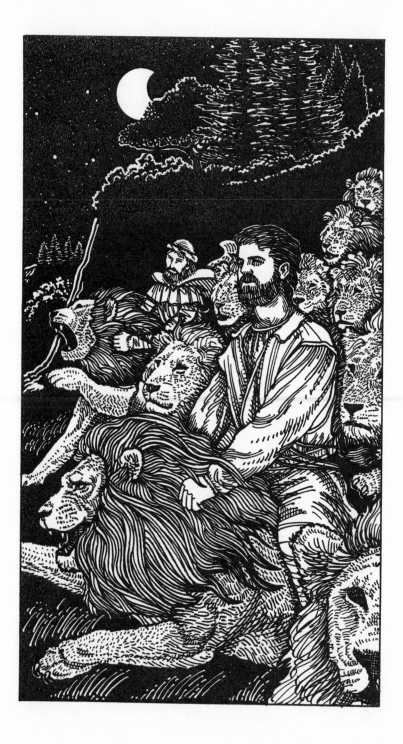

clearing and collapsed wherever they found room to fall. Their flanks heaved like sea breakers and their lungs thundered like waves exploding against the rocks. But all were content, and more—exhausted with joy and joyed with exhaustion.

"Are we in time?" gasped Lionheart.

"We are well in time to rescue your father."

They leaned their backs heavily against the rock, and Lionheart waited for the spinning in his head to go away. "Who won?" he finally thought to ask.

"We all did," answered Covenant.

Lionheart looked around him, remembering their first meeting here. "It is good that he shall not die here. This is a cursed place."

"Our work has lifted part of the curse," said Covenant, "but there have always been evil places in the land because there has always been evil in the hearts of the people."

"Could we not make this a place where none would ever come again?" Lionheart asked.

"Do you have an idea?" answered Covenant, with his own question. "A little terror of the right kind would do no harm," he added with a smile. "But," he continued to say without a smile, "they will find other ways to be rid of the ones they will not keep. Denying them the rock will make no difference in the end."

Lionheart murmured a few more questions, and Covenant nodded, smiling again. Most of the shaggy company slept; some watched. All waited with the men for something to happen.

* * *

Within an hour there came a noise from the path. Covenant waved his hand, and the lounging lions faded away into the night. Lionheart saw them becoming one with the shadows, laying themselves low after their rest.

"Here they come," breathed Lionheart. Someone was drawing near, someone trying to make little noise but still sounding sharp echoes and snapping through the forest.

And there on the path a woman struggled under the burden of a semiconscious man, an old man, thin and pale, with the snow of the years upon his head. Lionheart stirred anxiously but made no noise.

On the woman came, unaware of the host of lions lying quietly all around them. She turned her back to the unseen men and lowered her burden to the rock.

Covenant nudged Lionheart.

Lionheart stepped forward, tilted back his head and roared. The mighty sound shook the branches of the trees and brought a wild and wavering scream from the woman.

She plunged headlong into the clearing and stopped abruptly. The moon showed her a glade filled with lions—all alive, all alert, all looking at her with glowing eyes. Her heart beat wildly, but she had forgotten to breathe, and her limbs were frozen with fear.

Then Covenant stepped out from the trees and spoke to her. "We have come because this is an evil place. It is an evil place because you made it so."

She trembled at his voice but could not turn her head to him. She had never dreamed so many lions could be found in all the forests of the land, and now they were before her.

"As you have sent others to their doom," Covenant continued, "so your doom is before you.

"But we give you a single chance, which is one more than you spared either your daughter or your father." He gestured, and the mass of lions parted a narrow way for her feet.

"Run," Covenant commanded. "Run, and let us see how swiftly you can find shelter. Run! Or there will be no mercy for you at all."

She ran.

Not a lion twitched, though they watched her unblinkingly until she passed through the terrible, patient circle and reached the edges of the trees.

Then Lionheart roared again, and the lions leapt after her, with a single voice of outraged majesty and a multitude of angry feet.

She screamed as she ran, feeling their breath on her legs and their claws tearing at her clothes and their massive bodies snapping the branches aside.

The chase disappeared from sight, and Covenant said calmly, "She flies to her hut, where her man waits, but even he cannot grant her safety. He shall flee as well. He did nothing to stop her evil, and he will suffer with her. Terror is theirs this night, and teeth and tearing on every side, though they will not be harmed except through fear. They will be an agony of miles from here when the lions tire of the chase and begin to wander home."

"It is good that they should learn fear."

"If they do not learn a little fear now, they must learn more later." Covenant turned to watch Lionheart, who had picked up the limp form of his father. "Your sister will never return, either to this forest or to her home. No one will blame her.

"Long will the lions remember this night."

"And I as well," said Lionheart, embracing and supporting the unresisting form of his father. "All your words have come true."

"All the promises I gave to you are fulfilled," the beggar replied. "You shall see many more assurances kept in full before your work is done in Glory."

Only three lions were left, relaxing on the forest floor in the profound silence.

"Let us rest here for a few hours," said Covenant, urging Lionheart and his burden toward the lions. "We should wait until your father revives enough from the numbing powder to enjoy his ride." He smiled in the darkness as he helped them to comfortable positions against the lions' flanks. "No one will disturb us."

ELEVEN

Hammered Gold

BINDER CAME DOWNSTAIRS IN THE MORNING LIGHT AND found the ever-changing lady already at breakfast.

"Are you at ease here?" he asked gently.

She looked up at him with eyes that were momentarily the color of the sky, on their way from forest-brown to sea-green. "I am as much at ease here as I have ever been elsewhere," she said. "This is a very wonderful house."

"You fit in well, and I certainly find no offense in your presence. I am learning to look first for the cloak."

"You have been quite tolerant of me," she said. "Some people are drawn to me at first, but in the end they are driven away by the changes no one can control."

"I must be tolerant with all," replied Binder. "Or who would be tolerant with me?"

* * *

Day after day Trueteller came to the roof and found Farsight teetering on the edge of the bright tiles, face into the breeze and wings uplifted where the wind could sort his feathers. Then he would flutter up to her shoulder and submit to her attention and care.

"Soon," she whispered as she smoothed the feathers on his neck, "soon you will be ready."

Covenant found her there and joined her in admiring the eagle. "Farsight seems to be quite fond of you," he said. "Whenever I see him, you are there; wherever I find you, he is there on your shoulder. Does not his weight weary you?"

"No," she said, reaching up to first ruffle and then smooth his feathers. "I feel his weight, but it is not a great burden. I am no longer afraid of his beak, and I have sewn leather pads into my clothes to ease the terror of his talons. He responds to me kindly, but he is not a tame bird."

Farsight stretched out his wing to preen his feathers, and the sudden shade hid her face from the sun.

"I will miss him when he is well enough to fly."

"You would not keep him here?"

"I do enjoy him, but even if I could hold him to the earth, I would not. It would not be fair to him. He was made for the sky, not to live in the midst of people who would either ignore him or abuse him.

"I have enjoyed caring for him; it is like having a child again."

"You have many children in Lionheart's realm."

"The nursery? I love his charges and I am delighted by his work, but they are not my own flesh."

"Neither is Farsight, but he is healing nicely," Covenant said, reaching out to caress the mighty bird. "I think he will be ready to fly soon."

"Yes, he is ready. What do I do now?" she asked. "I have been patient and have asked you no questions about my husband."

"You have done well," replied Covenant, beaming his approval. "But more is required of you—now and later. For now, buy all the gold you can afford," Covenant said.

"Gold?" she asked. "I have never heard you ask for that before!"

"Gold," he repeated. "But not for me. It will buy you one of your wishes come true."

She thought for a moment. "I have no gold, but Candle has riches almost beyond measure, for you have blessed his shop . . ."

"I mean for you alone to do this, and to tell no one until it is done. You have your own store of silver coins and coppers now; it will be sufficient."

All the next morning Trueteller went about her task, buying fragments of gold quietly at various places throughout Glory.

She brought it back to Covenant. "My private riches have gathered me less than a handful of gold. Will it be enough?"

"It will," Covenant said. "Divide the gold into two equal piles, and hammer them flat into two bands. Make each one as wide as three fingers and as long as the stretch of your hand."

"I am not a metalsmith. My work is very poor."

"It will be sturdy and bright, and that is all that matters here."

That day and the next she labored clumsily in an isolated room in a quiet corner of the house, pounding and bending and filing. When she was done, her hands were scraped and blistered from the file, and bruised and stiff from the hammer. She bandaged the cuts, spread lotion on the bruises and brought her work to Covenant.

He examined her work. "You have done very well," he said. "And now for the rest," he continued as he gave them back to her. "Engrave a heart upon this band of gold, and embed my mark upon the other."

Trueteller nodded at the mention of Covenant's mark, for it lay all around them in his house. Then she shook her head in bewilderment over his request, but went to do as she had been told.

She returned later with the bands and yet another painful scratch from the awl. "These bands are too heavy for rings," she said. "What are they for?"

"They are heavy, but Farsight is strong; they will not slow him down."

"Farsight?"

"Yes. He shall bear a gift and a message both. Come, and you will see." They ascended to the roof, and Farsight came to them with a noisy but gentle greeting.

Covenant took the plates in his hands and bent them nearly into a circle with his powerful fingers. He held them up for Trueteller to see the marks on the outside, then slipped a band around each of Farsight's legs and squeezed them shut.

Farsight peered down at the bands and shook one foot experimentally, but he did not protest.

"Stroke him again and urge him on his way," said Covenant.

After a final caress she lifted the handsome bird and pitched him gently into the air. They bid the eagle goodbye as he lifted, circled, then beat away southward as though his destination were already fixed in his mind.

Covenant turned to her. "You asked me another question."

"I did?"

"You did. And in answer I say that you have been so absorbed with Farsight that you have not spoken to Moonflower for several days. I think she has a question for you that is also an answer."

Trueteller's eyes widened, and she set off breathlessly to find the daughter who had defied death.

She found her daughter sitting in the waning rays of the sun, sipping a brew of fragrant herbs and glowing as brightly as the sunset. Silently, Trueteller laid a trembling hand on

Moonflower's slim belly.

"Are you . . . ?" she asked.

"I may be," said Moonflower timidly. "What does it feel like?"

Twenty years fell away in a rush, and mother and daughter began a talk that lasted undisturbed into the night.

*   *   *

"I am a foolish old woman," confessed Trueteller to Wordsmith the next day. "Some of my worries and hopes must seem very selfish and shallow in Covenant's eyes."

Wordsmith shrugged. "Do not be too hasty to judge. It is no offense to be either old or a woman. We have all been foolish, and we are all being changed for the better."

TWELVE

The Voyage
of the
Childsbreath

COVENANT HELD COUNCIL WITH THEM ALL THE NEXT morning.

"You are a warrior," he said to Freeblade, "but you have never fought. We will make a journey together, and you shall anoint your blade with the blood of battle."

He turned. "Wordsmith, you shall come with us."

Beauty was crestfallen, though she hid it well. She clung to Wordsmith's arm and gazed at Covenant.

"Do not be afraid, Beauty," said Covenant. "I brought you to him from the rock of choosing, and brought him back to you from Rockhaven. Can I not bring him back to you again?"

She nodded.

"And I have not finished my words," he continued. "I am to go, and Freeblade and Wordsmith. And you, Beauty, shall go with us as well."

A startled expression came to her face, followed by delight. "I would be very pleased to go with you," she murmured. "Where are we going?"

"Back to the sea," Covenant said. "Binder and the Chameleon Lady shall stay here and look after the rest in our absence."

While they were pondering this, Covenant called Flamerider and Firecolt to him. "I have a gift for you two." He handed them a fired clay ornament on a plain metal chain. It puzzled the boys, for neither of them could tell exactly what it was. It was neither all man nor all animal, nor were they even certain that it was supposed to be alive. But it drew their eyes repeatedly, and they wondered what sort of magic it held.

"Take this," said Covenant, "and wear it always. One of you wear it today, and the other tomorrow, and in turns after that. This charm will save your lives—and more than your own lives. When you are called upon to deliver what you do not have, cast this ornament down and break it.

"Do not break it now, or lose it. But when you are threatened by the sword to deliver what you do not have, you must remember the provisions of Covenant."

They did not understand, but at a reassuring nod from Binder they bowed and returned to their seats.

Covenant dismissed them one by one, with a blessing.

Later, to the Chameleon Lady alone, he said, "Two days from now, when evening begins to fall, you must go to the palace and deliver your message to the king. After that, be surprised at nothing that happens," he added with a smile. "I know you are bright and full of courage; though you say little, you learn much and will do well at any task you set your heart to."

He told her what to say, and she began to see a glimmer of light in his ways.

* * *

The next morning, without fanfare, the four travelers left afoot for the distant sea, and soon they passed the village of the lepers.

"What is this place?" asked Freeblade.

"It is a town of lepers," said Beauty.

"Some call it Heartbreak," added Wordsmith.

"Why do you not visit there, Covenant?" asked Beauty. "Surely if any place needs your touch it is there." Wordsmith remembered his own like question.

"I would not be welcomed," Covenant said. "But I shall soon send someone there in my name, and my welcome shall come in its time."

"Who will be your messenger?" inquired Wordsmith.

"May I go?" asked Freeblade.

"Or I?" asked Beauty.

"No. You know too much. Ignorance—and innocence— would better suit my plans for this place."

"And I am neither ignorant nor innocent," said Wordsmith.

"Nor I," admitted Beauty.

"Once you were innocent, and even ignorant of your innocence. Now, however, you are only innocent of ignorance." Covenant smiled his enigmatic smile, and they went on.

For three days their feet conquered the miles, and they arrived at Graycove just before dusk. The company came to the house of Deedtester and were well received. Covenant left them alone there, and Joykeeper spoke to them in awed tones. The three travelers were surprised, but not astonished, by the work Covenant had done there.

When Covenant returned, he beckoned to Deedtester and Seaswallower and said, "The time has come to claim the *Childsbreath*—for a while, at least. There is an island to the west that I must visit."

The fisherman fell silent and looked at Covenant for a long moment before continuing. "There is only one island nearby, and you should not go there," he said gravely. "There are horrible things there."

Covenant answered him. "Sometimes the most horrible things are only those which have not been exposed to the light."

"What horrors have you seen?" asked Freeblade.

"Shadows. Many shadows," said the fisherman. "Even in the brightest light of day that island is dark. And moans—moans and wailing and screams of old, cold fear."

"Yet someone lives there?" asked Freeblade.

"There is life there, if you call existence living. None of us go to that fear-ridden place. I would not let the shadow of my boat touch the sand of that island."

"The *Childsbreath* is no longer yours to command," Covenant reminded him. "You bound her to me when I returned Seaswallower to you."

"She is yours, without argument. I tell you only what all folk here know and fear."

"This island?" asked Wordsmith. "Must we go there?"

"We should, we must, and we shall," answered Covenant. "It is, after all, part of this world. And even that island was shaped by the hand of the Elder God. You and your son will sail us there," he continued, turning to Deedtester, "but you need not leave the boat if you do not wish to."

They all slept where they could find room, either in the hut or on the sand outside, and they sailed with the dawn. The three with Covenant were delighted, for they had never been on the sea before. Beauty perched herself by the bow, exclaiming excitedly over the dolphins and whales that surfaced near the boat, and enjoying every drop of spray thrown aside by their passage.

At midday an island grew larger off the starboard bow. Seaswallower pointed, but it was hardly necessary. The gloomy pall that hung over the island marked it for all eyes to see.

Sailing closer in the lee of the island, they could see that

many of the shadows were actually the black stone walls of a sprawling, shabby building. Parts of the structure closest to the shore looked newer and more hastily built.

Freeblade hailed the silent shore, but there was no answer, no stir or motion. Nothing living could be seen except a few trees ringing the sand.

The bow of the *Childsbreath* crunched into the sand, and the four from Glory jumped down to wade in the warm surf to the dry land.

THIRTEEN

Haunted Rooms

The door to the rambling ruin gaped at them, and shadows tumbled out the unused doorway to greet them. Their footsteps violated the sand that had drifted deep over the sill.

Covenant lighted the torches in his hand. "Let us go inside," he said. "We will never conquer by standing here."

He stooped to enter the gloomy arch, but Freeblade prevented him, saying, "You have appointed me Warrior. Where there may be danger, I should go first."

Covenant smiled and stepped back and motioned him inside. "Once you dreaded the shadows, but now your courage controls your fears. You have grown from fearful to fearless."

"No," he said. "This book has soaked so deep into my soul that there is no more room for fear, save the fear that I would be unworthy of the name Freeblade."

He plunged into the darkness with his sword held high and with Covenant behind him. Beauty and Wordsmith followed silently and not without misgivings.

"Which way?" whispered Freeblade.

"Any direction you wish," said Covenant. "Any path will lead us to the one who lives here."

They began the long task of searching room to room. The darkness yielded reluctantly to their torches; cobwebs bloomed from the corners, shrouding everything in a veil of gray. The rooms seemed to spiral back into each other, and Beauty was sure they had crossed several rooms more than once. Some looked ancient and fine but abandoned, while some had been built in clumsy haste and now lay half-open to the wind.

Beauty was keenly aware of a disquieting presence, an unpleasant aura in every room—a weight of shadows not sparked solely from the absence of the sun.

Three of them jumped when a voice split the darkness. Only Covenant seemed unaffected.

"Who's there?" cried someone in a cracked and hysterical quaver. "Who's there, I say?"

"Your friends," replied Covenant.

"There are no friends here," called the voice. "You are all my enemies. Be gone, you ghosts and shadows! I will give you no more harbor!" The words were brave enough but uttered with a hollow hope, as though they had been uttered in vain many times before.

"We are not ghosts," said Covenant, "and neither are we shadows. Come forth and see!"

A wrinkled, pale man slowly crept into the circle of their torches. His matted white hair and dirty beard hung long and weary about his face.

"Who are you?" he asked again, his voice dry and cracked from long disuse.

"We come in the name of the Elder God," said Freeblade

boldly, but then he did not know how to continue.

Covenant picked up the thread. "We have come to deliver you from your prison. You have lived in the darkness too long."

"You know of me?" asked the man.

"I do," replied Covenant, "but none of my friends know what this house is, or how it came to be. They should hear that story directly from your lips."

The man stared at them uncertainly. Beauty sensed his discomfort and stepped forward. "He is Covenant, who leads us—the man of true and certain promises," said Beauty. "The man with the sword is Freeblade, and this is my husband, Wordsmith. I am called Beauty."

"Put your blade away," said the man, "or I will go where you cannot find me."

Covenant agreed. "Put it away, Freeblade. The danger here is not to us but to this man."

Freeblade promptly sheathed his sword. The man relaxed visibly and drifted near enough to press Wordsmith's arm between his fingers. "You *are* real—not phantoms, at least," he said. "Though you can do nothing to deliver me, I would not turn you away, for I do not remember the last visitor to this place."

He backed away, and they followed him deeper into the labyrinth of rooms. They eventually made a series of sharp turns, and then blinked and shielded their eyes from the sudden beams of sunlight slanting through holes in the roof.

The man stopped abruptly, and they found themselves standing in a rough stone room tacked on to the very edge of a cliff that tumbled down to the restless waters below. The other rooms had been bare and hollow, but this one was stuffed with stacks of old books and drawings, a pile of shabby clothes, a store of nuts and herbs and dried fish, a brush pallet on the dirt floor, and a tiny fire glowing in a makeshift fireplace. The walls gaped widely, and sundogs played together at their feet.

Covenant sat on the floor, and the others joined him. "Tell us your name," he said, "and how it is that you dwell here with ghosts."

"That is no secret," the hermit said sadly, shifting his slight weight from one hip to the other. "I am Grimshade. Once I had a family here and many friends, and all this island was mine—until my words and my deeds overcame the love that struggled to blossom from my heart. In the end I drove my loved ones away. To my sorrow, the shadows of my deeds and the woe of my words did not go with them, but stayed to haunt me and drive me down with the constant specter of the past I cannot change and the future I cannot avoid.

"I built a new room to my house and dwelt there where no horrid echoes lived. But every deed I performed, every word I said created a new shadow, a fresh dark ghost. And the ghosts would not leave me alone. When that room, too, was filled with shadows, I built another new room for myself."

"Until it, too, filled with ghosts," said Freeblade.

"Yes," the hermit said sadly, "that always happens. The shadows come, like silt, like the slow soil of dark flood tides. I cannot stop them; I might as well dream of halting the gloom that follows the sunset. I used to go to my wishing well, to toss in my coins and appeal to the gods for release. But there were no gods there—only ghosts, more ghosts.

"I have summed the shadows and seen that their end is death. But the ghosts don't die. That is the curse of this house."

"Give me authority over these rooms," said Covenant quietly.

"These rooms are yours to command," he replied, "but all of them are full of shadows." He slumped fully onto his pallet.

"Yes," said Covenant, "and all of them are angry."

He turned to Freeblade. "Slay the shadows," he ordered. "They are your first enemy and a fierce one. They are only the truth, but they have been given false life and power. It is not so dangerous to you as it will be difficult and exhausting."

Covenant turned to Grimshade. "And you must go with him—to name the ghosts as you find them. They were born of your words and deeds and must be owned by you again before they can be destroyed."

Grimshade stared at him. "That path carries more shame than I can carry. If I could defeat the shadows myself, I would have done so long ago."

"Yes, there is shame in proclaiming their names," answered Covenant, "but you will have shame forever if you do not defy them. You will do what you can, and Freeblade will do what you cannot.

"Destroy the first shadow that you fall upon," Covenant ordered Freeblade, "and let its dying blood run across the floor where we can see it. Bring the love of life to this place again."

"There is no love in this house," said the hermit. "Perfect fear casts out love."

"Yes, but perfect love casts out fear," Beauty replied.

With a great cry, Freeblade stood, drew his sword and plunged into the labyrinth. He was back in an instant, grasping a dark something that wiggled frantically in his fingers. "Name him," he commanded. Grimshade reluctantly uttered its foul name, and Freeblade struck his blade into the captive darkness; it spouted black blood as it shrieked and shriveled and vanished into nothingness.

Beauty blanched but did not turn away.

"That is only the first," said Freeblade, satisfied.

They returned to the ghost-swept rooms, and Beauty thought the gloom had lessened, as though the shadows were already retreating. Freeblade did not return with the second shadow, but slew it where they found it and went on to the next. The sounds of combat were clear to the company—Grimshade gleefully naming the ghosts as they were captured, Freeblade smiting with the blade and leaving destruction in his path. The uproar drifted back to them from ever-widening circles, both horrifying and fascinating them.

Time passed with no way to measure it until Freeblade, drenched in sweat and stumbling with happy weariness, returned, slumped on the floor and gazed at Covenant. "It was not a fair fight," he said. "They were not armed with any weapon that could touch me."

"But they were strong and fierce," replied Covenant, "and almost without number, were they not? It was a hard task and well done. You have always found favor in my eyes, and now you have found honor as well."

The house lay silent but light and airy; there were no dark ghosts left to shuffle and shade and moan. Where once shadows had clustered too thickly to be penetrated, now sunbeams found the cracks in the stone and danced on the floor.

Covenant turned to Grimshade, standing white-faced and weak with surprise and relief. "Your old name no longer fits you," observed Covenant.

"I never had love for that name," he answered.

"Then let your old name vanish with the ghosts. I would give you your new name now, but you have not learned enough to bear it. This is a nameless island," continued Covenant. "Are you content to be, for now, a nameless man on a nameless island?"

"As you wish," said the hermit dazedly. "My name is of little import to me; there is no one to call it aloud. You have, indeed, slain the shadows, and I am grateful beyond words. How can I serve you in return?"

"You can serve me by staying here," said Covenant. "You are the final man in the west, and the man who last hails each day's setting sun: to you shall come the first sight of the final fires."

"What must I do?"

"You have a treasure to find, and afterward I will send Wordsmith and Freeblade for you."

"Treasure?" He looked both interested and puzzled. "The only treasure left here is solitude."

"Think again. You have lived here a very long time, and perhaps fear has driven out fond memories."

The hermit thought. "There used to be . . . or was I dreaming? A special room where I knew peace and contentment . . . but that was long ago, before the shadows came. I can scarcely remember it."

"You should find it, then," said Covenant. And with a warm farewell he led the others out to the waiting *Childsbreath*.

* * *

"And now what?" asked the tired Freeblade, watching the receding island and the waving figure upon the sand.

"Now we return to Glory," answered Covenant. "We have done what we sailed to do."

"All this voyage for one man?" asked Wordsmith.

"Is the end of the earth too far to go for any such one who needs our help?" countered Covenant.

"No," agreed Wordsmith, "of course not."

"Then the road beckons us home again."

"Covenant," asked Freeblade later, "was Grimshade in his right mind?"

"He was very nearly out of it forever," replied Covenant. "Silence and suffering will do that to one who stands alone against familiar and fearsome terrors."

He turned away to Beauty, who had again found a seat at the bow and was absorbing every sight and sound of the ocean.

"Covenant," she said, "can anything be better than this?"

"Yes. This is good, very good, but there is better yet that is far beyond your imagination. You shall have that someday soon, with no need to imagine. The great sorrow is that much worse than this will fall upon you before the best of all comes to stay."

She sought an explanation from him, but she was answered only by silent sadness.

FOURTEEN

The
Clear Purple
Miracle

Not even cold water from the mountain streams could soothe the fever of the King. He burned and flamed in its grip, sweating his life away into nothingness, while his advisors and physicians looked on helplessly. Their worry weighed heavy upon them and them alone, for they kept the news of the royal sickness from the people of the land.

Each day the King staggered to the mirror, only to be faced with the slow approach of his death. His only ease came when sleep overrode the suffering, but sleep was elusive, and even in his sleep he was not left alone. His dreams boiled in his brain, blurring the boundary between life and madness.

Until the night a long-haired shadow came to the palace and walked unheeded past the guards. Nor did the servants hinder her as she drifted through the innermost chambers to stand before the ailing King.

She spoke, and he roused, hearing the voice and beholding the face of his own Queen.

*   *   *

With the pale morning light, he burst from his chambers and yelled for his advisors. "I have had a dream!" he called hoarsely. "A vision, a promise, an oracle, a sign! Bring me the master-at-arms, quickly now, for my strength is fading."

He sweltered upon his purple pillows until the soldier returned. Though his fever still raged high, he spoke firmly and steadily, with only a slight trace of weakness in his voice.

"Send men, and find for me in Glory two youths, dressed in red and blue, playing in the street. Bring them, just as you find them, and come back in haste. I have had a vision, and these boys shall give me new life. Now go. At once!"

At noon Firecolt and Flamerider were gaming before the house while Binder and the Chameleon Lady rested on the steps and watched.

Their attention was diverted by a soldier riding slowly down the narrow street, gazing intently at the children he encountered.

"What does *he* want?" whispered Binder. "We don't see *them* down here often."

"I think I know," she whispered. "Watch and see."

The rider reined in his horse when he saw Firecolt and Flamerider. He watched them closely and then dismounted. The boys stopped their play and watched him in return, their attraction to the horse tempered by their awe of the man and suspicion of his power.

"You are their parents?" he called to the adults.

Binder hesitated less than a heartbeat. "They are our boys."

"The King has called them to do his bidding."

"What? Why does he need them?" flared Binder.

"I explain nothing," said the soldier, "for nothing is explained to me. The King says go, and I go; he says bring them, and I bring them. What are their names?"

The boys had retreated up the steps and were huddling close to the adults. The Chameleon Lady nudged them with her knee.

"Be polite, boys. Tell him your names."

"I am Firecolt," said the boy in blue.

"And I am Flamerider," added the boy in red.

"Come with me," the rider said.

"They are staying here," Binder said flatly.

"You will not let them go?" asked the soldier.

"No!"

"Then you must answer to the King."

"And who will answer to me if something happens to them?" thundered Binder.

The Chameleon Lady tugged at Binder's arm. "Let them go," she whispered. "This is Covenant's doing and not evil at work."

Binder could not prevent the soldier and wisely did not try; the frightened boys were lifted up on the saddle before the rider, and the horse carried them away without delay.

In only a few short minutes the confused, apprehensive lads were ushered into the King's presence. The King motioned for his attendants and messengers to leave, saying, "I wish to speak with them alone." Then, turning to the youths, he began, "Lads, you can see that I am ill and weakened. Last night I had a vision, a visit. My Queen came to me and put in my head a picture of two boys enjoying the freedom of the streets, even as my messengers found you. Her voice said to me, 'Find the boys, and send them in the name of the Elder God, for in this bottle one may find life and healing. With its discovery your land and people will be blessed and healed and will become great again.'

"And then I saw you walking together on a dusty road, making a long journey. You came to a far village and went to a certain wineseller's shop marked with a wooden star above the door. You entered and gave the merchant a token.

"He delivered to you a bottle; you padded it with old cloth wrappings and made your way hastily from that place. My Queen showed me no more than that and made no explanations, but I know in my great wisdom what it intended. You will go and find this miraculous bottle of wine; with it I shall heal myself, and this land will know again the peace and prosperity that only I can bring it. I command you to go now, and tell no one of your purpose. No one. Even my advisors will be kept ignorant, for this act must be done in secret.

"You carry a pledge—a sign or token. Show it to me, that I may confirm you are the ones. Now."

They looked at each other, puzzlement and fear fighting for the upper hand in their eyes.

"I do not have it, so you must. Show it to me now, or suffer my wrath!"

Firecolt finally found his voice. "Covenant," he said to his brother faintly. "Remember Covenant. It is your day to wear his charm."

Flamerider removed the chain from his neck and offered it to the King.

"This is no token," he snarled. "Do not play me for a fool." He hurled it back at them. Both boys grabbed for it and missed, and it shattered on the paved stones of the floor.

Flamerider plucked something shiny from the debris.

"That is it!" shouted the King. "Let me see it!"

"It is only half a copper," said the disappointed boy, handing it over.

"I do not care what it is or where it came from or what it means," snapped the weakened King, "as long as you can trade it for that bottle." He caressed the bent and broken coin before handing it back. "You have a mission," he continued. "Go and do it, faithfully, fearlessly, and quickly. The well-being of this land hangs upon your success—as does your own well-being. I advise you not to fail."

The King sank back onto his bed and tugged on a rope to summon his attendants. His eyes closed as the boys were led out of the room.

Then the gates clanged shut behind them, and they were left alone—with half a copper and a mission, but no guide or directions.

"What are we to do?" whispered Flamerider.

"We must tell Binder," murmured Firecolt.

They ran all the way to Covenant's house and blurted out their story to Binder and the Chameleon Lady.

Binder was amazed and indignant until the lady explained her part in the matter. "It was frightening, but exciting, to do Covenant's bidding and see it unfold exactly as he prophesied.

"Let them go," she continued. "These boys are half men already, and two half-men may do the work of one man."

"But there is still a whole *boy* left over," replied Binder.

"Then the man will take care of the boy, and the boy will keep the man alert," she replied.

Her serenity helped convince him, and he thought for a moment before speaking. "Wordsmith has told me of a miracle of wine and water that he witnessed along the road to Glory, a miracle that happened shortly after he joined with Covenant. I know that road. There are signs along the way, and it will be difficult to become lost." He gave the boys clear directions. "A word of warning: don't go near the towns, and be sure to watch for thieves along the way. There are also many lepers in that first village. It can barely be seen from the road, and you would do well to stay away from there."

With trust striving for the upper hand in their hearts, Binder and his helper provisioned the boys, blessed them and walked with them to the gate of Glory.

Firecolt and Flamerider bade them goodbye and moved off down the road.

"Everyone's away now," said the Chameleon Lady, the reality of their sudden departure dawning upon her. "I believe in

Covenant, but I'm not sure I will sleep soundly until all these travelers are at home again."

"Keep remembering Covenant," said Binder. "As you said, they are about *his* errands."

The afternoon was bright with sun, and the evening was illuminated by the moon. The boys avoided Heartbreak without incident and did not stop until much later when the silver ball sank behind the mountains.

When they paused and sat against a tree to make their meager supper, they could see the very tiny lights of the King's palace glinting on one of the mountain peaks. The lights did not comfort them as they slept. When their hunger woke them in the morning, they ate and continued on their way with caution and misgivings.

Ever watchful, they slipped through the fields and barren rocky places and across a river. On the far side of the bank, Firecolt halted and pulled Flamerider into the shadows of the trees.

"We are being followed," he said softly.

"I know," answered Flamerider. "I can feel it, though I see nothing." They listened, and Flamerider began again, "Why did Covenant send us for this task? We are from Glory; we do not know the ways of the woods."

"Covenant must have his reasons," replied Firecolt, "or Binder and the lady would not have let us come. And Covenant knows that we know the ways of the wilderness inside our stone walls. Life is not so much different out here."

They waited.

Nothing crossed the river behind them. They heard nothing, saw nothing, but felt the eyes of the watcher upon them.

They hurried on.

And that evening they saw a lion. It watched them from a distance, and seemed content. The boys wondered if Lionheart had sent it.

As they prepared for sleep in the crooks of an old tall tree, their sense of the unseen eyes lessened somewhat. But in the night a horrible roar awakened them, and they huddled in the darkness while a savage fight tore the night. After an unmeasured time of terror, the sounds died away into a grisly mashing and crunching. Then even that stopped.

They waited open-eyed for the dawn, even though the sensation of being followed had completely vanished. In the new light they saw a bloody, trampled area where two mighty animals had contended. One had torn apart the other, and the victor had feasted and padded away, leaving lion marks in the dirt.

The two boys looked at the abandoned carcass. "I do not know what kind of beast this was," said Flamerider. "Those teeth and claws are horrors."

"Nor do I," added Firecolt, "but I am glad it is dead."

They looked at each other. "I think we have been protected," said Firecolt. "Let us go before another one comes."

* * *

The next two days held less adventure and little fear. The road was empty save a few merchants' caravans of goods, and the boys hid each time until the dust had settled again. Orchards and fields, visited in the dead of night, supplied them with ample nourishment when their food ran out.

The journey seemed to drag on forever, but at last they came over the rise of a small hill and saw an isolated building in the distance, just as Binder had described. As they drew closer, they confirmed that the wooden sign over the door was the one they had been seeking.

It was dim inside, and neither boy could see at first the aged proprietor who spoke to them from the depths of the gloom. Firecolt handed him the carefully kept token without saying a word. Then he looked around him, his eyes growing accustomed to the dark, and he saw, lining the walls, rack upon wooden rack filled with dustily gleaming bottles.

The wineseller looked thoughtfully at the token, turning it

over in his long fingers. "I know this coin," he said. "He ruined the rest, and now he claims the last bottle?" He expected no answer, and received none. "Good riddance," he continued in a surly voice. "I am weary of answering questions about one dusty bottle on the mantle, and even more weary of seeing it every day. I don't know why I kept it, but I did. I suppose I was afraid *he* would come back again if I didn't." He reached down a solitary bottle from over the fireplace and handed it to the boys. "Take the wine—or water, or whatever it is—and leave the half of the copper to me. I have its mate and will not let it sit idle." Respect and resentment mixed in his voice.

"If you please, sir, we need something to wrap it in."

He threw them some old cloths and cursed them. The fire twins stumbled out into the broad daylight, having said little and done less, but with most of their task complete.

Or so they thought.

So far the King's vision had proven true, but Firecolt was beginning to doubt. He did not understand how restoring the King to health would make the land prosperous again. The land would only suffer longer under him, and the people would be forced to wait a few years more for a new and perhaps better king to be crowned.

These thoughts returned to his mind again and again on the journey home, and he discussed them with Flamerider. Neither could reach an understanding or a conclusion.

They sensed nothing unusual on their return journey, but they did find fresh lion tracks at odd intervals. They were comforted and walked on with light hearts.

When they knew they were nearing Glory, they decided to travel through that night and be home by dawn. But while they slipped through a field in search of fruit, something snagged Firecolt's ankle and he fell. He started to rise again, but a pair of sweaty, dirty hands pushed him to the ground and wrestled away his belongings.

"What have we here?" a man growled. "Two boys. Travel-

ing alone? I'm sure they'll want to share their food with me, and I wonder what's in the package?" The man broke off suddenly, coughing with great convulsions that shook his body. Then the moon came out in full, and Firecolt could see that the man was a leper. One leg was badly withered and twisted beneath him, and there was scarcely more than bone beneath the skin. He coughed again, and the rasping sound tore at his throat. He clawed at Firecolt's food sack, shoving the boy roughly to one side. Flamerider pounded on the man's side without effect until Firecolt told his brother to quit.

Firecolt rose to his feet and lunged for his belongings, but the wiry, wary leper ducked and knocked him down.

"You can't have that! It's ours!"

"It's as much mine as yours, little ones. But if you like you can both sit there and watch me eat."

"You can have the food. Just give us the package!"

"Oh, so it's that important, is it? Let's see what's inside." He unwrapped the bottle and held it in the air, where it sparkled in the moonlight. "Yes, yes. Wine. And a favored kind at that."

"But you can't have that either! It's the King's!"

"Then let the King come and take it away from me. I'm thirsty." He pulled out the stopper with one quick motion and said, "I won't be rude; I will at least drink to his health." He began to empty the bottle with greedy gulps. Firecolt lunged at him, but the leper scuttled away with his good leg and said, "Careful, boy. I wouldn't want to hurt you."

He continued drinking, long after Firecolt thought he had reached the bottom of the bottle.

"My thanks to you, boy. This is the finest stuff I've had in a long time." His voice was beginning to sound unsteady, and some of his words were not quite plain. The deep coughing was not as bad now—he seemed to be swallowing his pain with the drink. He took another series of long gulps, looking with concern and puzzlement at the bottle each time he lowered it. "This is mighty powerful stuff," he murmured. "How did they get so much of it in one little bottle?"

Firecolt and Flamerider slipped away into the shadows and watched where the crippled outcast could not see them. Presently, that reclining figure lowered the bottle and laid his head on the ground. Firecolt crept up and took the bottle away. The leper made a feeble grasp at the wine, then rolled on his side and slept. Firecolt glanced at him, then looked down at the crippled leg. Even as he watched, the flesh around the bone began to fill out; the bone lengthened, and soon Firecolt could no longer tell that it had once been withered. The man breathed clearly and easily now, without the slightest trace of a cough, and his skin innocent of the hateful white bloom.

Firecolt checked the bottle and received another shock. The bottle was full. He poured some on the ground. The level did not change. He found the stopper and pushed it in. Without looking at the bottle again, he gathered their things and ran with Flamerider at his heels.

Far away and safe, they stopped and sprawled out on the grass to rest. Firecolt's mind was still running fast, and he panted, "This wine *can* heal."

"Just like the King said," whispered Flamerider.

They rose as soon as their hearts beat normally again. The moon was almost gone in the west as they left the fringes of Heartbreak. But even after the town of sickness lay behind them, one particular sound still echoed in their ears: the sound of a child in great pain. Not the wail of a child woken suddenly in the night, but the constant wearied crying of one who could not understand why its misery would not go away. And the light breeze brought them the answering, soothing sound of a woman's voice as she sang softly, but in vain, to her child.

Firecolt looked up and saw the pinpoint lights in the mountains far ahead. Suddenly he remembered the King and heard him as he spoke. "The voice came to me, saying, 'In this bottle one may find life and healing. With its discovery your land and people will be blessed and healed and will become great again.'

Then my vision ended."

Firecolt stopped in the road and listened very hard to his thoughts. *The land will be healed. The vision had said nothing about the King. The King, even if he were healed, would not help the land. The people will be healed. The wine in this bottle can heal.* He looked up at the mountains again, and he knew that unless they hurried they would be too late. He considered the image of the King speaking low from his deathbed, and he thought about the echo of the child's crying.

He whispered to Flamerider, and they turned and ran back to Heartbreak.

A watchman stopped them, surprised that anyone would venture near. "Lions raid at night, but not boys," he said. "Why are you here?"

He unraveled the thread of the story from Firecolt's tangled narrative, but was doubtful of the claim. He called others, and soon a host of lepers surrounded them.

"Is this true?" growled one of the men.

"Yes! I saw it happen," insisted Firecolt.

The man took the bottle from Firecolt, uncorked it and held the tip to his nose. "It smells like wine," he said. He spilled a splash onto his hand and tasted it gingerly. "It tastes like wine," he said, "but just in case, you drink some first. There are people around who would gladly poison a leper."

Firecolt drank and grimaced at the strength of the liquid. Then he held the bottle up and waited. Everyone watched, but nothing happened.

Another man snatched the bottle away. "I'll chance it," he rumbled. "It might cure me, or it might kill me, or it might do nothing at all. But I'd rather have a quick death than this slow rot."

He drank, and waited, and in moments his changed body proved the truth of Firecolt's words.

A riot of shouting and guzzling and healing broke out, while the boys huddled on the ground avoiding the turmoil of the tattered boots and bare feet.

Then the lepers hastened to the square in Heartbreak, yelling the town awake. The bottle, still not quite empty, passed from hand to hand and house to house.

What had begun as a solitary challenge in the darkness became a shared joy among friends. "Has everyone had their fill of this potion?" shouted the man who had taken charge. "No man too old, no woman too shy, no child too small!" A few last children were handed to him, and he filled their tiny mouths and watched their flesh purify as they sputtered and gasped and protested with wordless wails the strong taste of the wine.

He handed the bottle back to Flamerider. Firecolt then took it and shook it experimentally. He tipped it over his palm. Nothing came out. "It is empty," he said.

The boys, too tired to walk again, and now fearful of the King if he heard of their disobedience, slept in the shadows while the people lit fires and danced and sang.

A woman shook them awake in the midst of the celebration. "Who gave you this bottle? Whose wine is this?" she asked.

"It is Covenant's," answered Firecolt sleepily.

"Who is Covenant?" she asked.

"Come to Glory and see," Flamerider invited.

And they did. By the time the morning light fell upon their faces, every person in the village—now whole and healthy— was prepared. Some walked, some rode donkeys, others rode with their wrapped burdens in one ancient cart. Groups of eight men took turns pulling it; the axles screamed in protest at every turn of the wheels, and the boys doubted it would last even the short journey to Glory.

Where there had been a colony of lepers, there was now a procession of whole people; where there had been a pool of human misery there were now only empty huts.

The boys led the former lepers back to Glory, leaving a joyfully abandoned village behind them.

FIFTEEN

The Men Who Would Be King

Beauty, Wordsmith and Covenant drew near to Glory and found the marks of many feet on the road before them. Outside the main gate they found an old, gaunt cart leaning against a tree and all but abandoned.

A man was unloading a final bag from the cart and hoisting it up on his shoulder. He looked up at the travelers staring at the wagon. "It is yours now," he said cheerfully, "if you want it. We have no more use for it."

"We?" asked Wordsmith.

"We." He waved his hand excitedly at himself and the tracks of the many feet in the dust. "We who are no longer lepers. Take the cart—we need it not. We have come in search of this Covenant who sent us the wondrous wine." Then he was gone.

"We accept your gift," said Covenant gravely to the empty silence.

"I do not understand," said Wordsmith.

"You don't have to," answered Covenant.

"But they're looking for you," said Beauty.

"They will find me soon enough. They are already heading toward the house."

"Lepers? What wine?" asked Freeblade.

Covenant only smiled. "You will all hear their story first-hand," he said. "Others of our company have been active in our absence."

"And what about this?" Wordsmith gestured to the sagging hulk of the wagon. The harness and reins lay on the ground, a hopeless tangle of discarded leather. "If it rolls for another dozen leagues, I will be surprised," said Wordsmith. "What shall we do with it? It is too wide for our narrow streets."

His speech was interrupted by the sounds of many trumpets blaring low and mournfully in the streets of Glory.

They hurried through the gates to hear that the King was dead.

"You knew this would happen, didn't you?" accused Wordsmith.

"Yes," said Covenant simply.

"And you did not tell us?" asked Beauty.

"You would only have worried," said Covenant, "and all the worry in the world would not have helped you."

Freeblade straightened his weary shoulders. "Then let us go and meet the lepers. They are alive, it seems, and can be tended to, while the King is beyond our help."

They approached the House of Covenant, and Binder met them at the door with news of the journey of the fire twins. Wordsmith, in turn, brought them details of the King's death.

The house was full of joyful, anxious strangers. As Covenant entered, Firecolt called out his name and sparked a flame of emotion that swept from room to room. Everyone tried to draw near, talking at once, and Binder was stunned by the happy pandemonium.

But Covenant was beaming. He climbed the stairs partway, turned, and somehow steered the crowd toward order with only his voice and visage.

"I know your story," he thundered, when the dying din had eased their ears. "This gift of wine was directed by the hand of the Elder God and accomplished in his name. It has had its full effect, I see. You are healed, and you are here, but what shall you do next?"

No one answered, for no one had considered the question yet.

"Why, make a new life in Glory," said one man finally.

"We will follow you," said a woman with children clinging to her skirts.

"Then go out into Glory," Covenant proclaimed, "and go with my blessing. Or stay here, and stay with my blessing. I need not speak to you now, but you will hear more of me in days to come. Should you face difficulties when I am not in this house, you must turn to Wordsmith, Beauty or Freeblade." He pointed them out to the multitude.

"Binder," he called, "is there food for a midday Feast?"

"Of course there is," answered Binder. "We seldom tend your house in vain."

So a Feast was held, and merry was the house, although black flags flew above the palace.

* * *

At the end of the afternoon, Covenant gathered the ones who knew him best and led them on a slow walk in the great amphitheater before the palace. He sat them down in the sand and stared at the palace.

"What happens now?" asked Lionheart, breaking the uneasy silence.

"What has always happened when a king dies heirless," answered Covenant, "though it has not happened in many lifetimes. People will choose champions for themselves, and there will be a tournament—an open court of armed combat. He who survives will be king."

"I did not know about these things," said Lionheart.

"My book told tales of this," said Freeblade. "I never dreamed I would witness such a combat myself."

Freeblade felt the weight of Covenant's gaze upon him, and soon he saw that the others were watching him too.

"Freeblade," said Covenant, "I bid you contend for this company."

Freeblade bowed. "Those who fail die." His eyes were both troubled and proud.

"Are you not prepared to die?" asked Covenant.

"I am prepared," replied Freeblade, "but I am not pleased to throw my life down for the mere trophy of a kingship. Is this a good thing that you bid me do? You have had no taste for violence before, nor have I ever heard that you wish for a crown."

"I shall not be the next king," Covenant said, "but I shall be the final one."

"I do not understand him," whispered Beauty to Wordsmith. "He speaks in riddles."

"Why should this time differ from all the rest?" Wordsmith whispered back.

"I cannot envision you with a sword in your hand," Freeblade said to Covenant. "But I was born for the blade, and I will fight for you."

"It is not the first battle you have fought for this company—nor will it be the last. And above that, I named you Champion of the House of Covenant."

"The night you gave me this name," Freeblade finished quietly. "I remember, and I will not dishonor either the name or the duty.

"When I win, you shall be king."

Covenant nodded. "That I shall, but perhaps the moment is

farther away than you think. And we may have differing ideas of victory. Nevertheless, you shall begin your task here tomorrow when the champions are named and the tournament begins." He turned to speak to them all again. "This peace in Glory has been kept—and opposed—by unseen hands," he said. "The end of all things shall come before you know peace like this again. It is a fragile thing, and not even the King's peace lasts forever."

"There is a legend," said Binder, "that as long as the judgment rock stands, we will still have peace." He pointed to the single jut of stone that overlooked the arena. Stairs were carved into its side, that one could stand on its lofty top and utter words of law and justice.

"Some legends have much truth in them," agreed Covenant.

And with that the council ended.

SIXTEEN

Rivals
and
Champions

FREEBLADE PULLED BINDER ASIDE. "COME WALK WITH ME," he said. "I would see the town with you from the top of the walls."

They left the others there in the street and climbed the long stairs to the broad walk on the wall.

Glory was quiet before them, but restless and afraid beneath the stillness. Few mourned for the king; most were awed by the presence of royal death; a few laid plans of their own and waited for the tournament.

"You did not call me out here to see the sights of Glory," Binder said, "for we have seen them many times before. Speak your mind. I am ready to listen."

"I know what is in your heart," said Freeblade quietly, "for the same thoughts have sounded in mine."

Binder stared at him. "The lady?"

"The same. Are you ready to dare the curse for her sake?"

"I believe I am," Binder answered, "but I will not fight you for her."

"You are right," replied Freeblade, "for I will not strive with you over her." He drew his sword from its sheath and looked at it with a mixture of affection and fear. "This is my bride and my burden, my calling and my companion. As much as I wish it, I should not have another distraction in my life.

"But we are both presumptuous, aren't we?" he chuckled. "I do not know that she would consent to either of us." He looked up at Binder. "I have had an adventure already," he said, "and they are only just beginning. But this could be the greatest adventure of all—to discover a woman who has been lost for years.

"I wish to have her," he continued, "but it is not good that I do, whether she wants me or not. I have looked at my own heart, and my motives are all too plain to me. I would take her as my own, not so much because I love her but because I love more the noble gesture. You, I think, are ready to care for her whether anyone sees or not."

"But is she ready to care for me?"

"You have spent much time with her," said Freeblade. "Enough to know her well."

"Enough to believe that I love her," Binder said firmly.

"It is still her choice—but we should see Covenant first."

* * *

When the two found Covenant, they laid their desires, their dialogue and their decisions before him.

"You have changed my life," said Binder, "and I have done little to repay you. Would this choice please you, that I extend your kindness and protection to another?"

"This is not enough to repay me," answered Covenant. "It cannot even begin to count against that debt. What you owe me is so great a debt that you will not begin to discharge it before time itself has lost its meaning. Nor is it even payment to me."

"I thought you would be pleased," said Freeblade, puzzled.

"I am," said Covenant, "but the gift Binder gives is to her, and not to me. I am most pleased that you settled it between yourselves in friendship and honor, and did not bring strife into this house."

He turned to Binder again and gently waved Freeblade from the room. "You have been bidden to do many things," he began, "and you will be bidden again. This act is not demanded of you, and I will not make you any false promises. Yes, it would please me, but you would fire no anger if you turned this chance away. It lies at your hand if you choose, but you can not choose to have—you can only choose to offer. I give you leave to love her, if you dare.

"You must make your decision, and soon, for she has a decision to make as well."

"But why should this privilege be mine? I have done only a single act of goodness," said Binder, "and you have loved me anyway."

"You were welcome here with or without an act of bravery. When you pulled the two boys from the fire, your moment of bravery was decided upon and committed and paid for and over in a few moments. But this choice requires courage and resolution, and not merely bravery. There is no hurry to act, and you will bear the price of your decision during every day that comes after."

"I will walk for a while, and think," said Binder.

"Take the lady with you to help you think," Covenant suggested with his wry, warm smile.

And within the space of a half hour Binder and the Chameleon Lady were walking the broad walls where the two rival friends had walked before. Binder was ill at ease, and did not know if it was a comfort that she walked so close beside him and waited contentedly for his words.

"Freeblade and I have spoken of you," he began carefully, "and it is our joint desire that you be cared for and be happy. If we could, we would gladly free you from your curse. But neither of us are magic men—even though Freeblade wields a holy sword, he casts no spells and breaks none."

"I have given up hope of being free from this parade of faces," she said. "I will be satisfied with an ordinary miracle."

"What would that be?"

"My desires have changed but little," she stated, turning to face him squarely. "I still long to be loved, as my sister was, but I will be loved only by an honorable man." Her eyes, gray at the moment, regarded him with a longing that could no longer be concealed.

"Lady," Binder said, "I have enjoyed your company more than I once enjoyed my books, though I did not think such a thing was possible." He took a deep breath. "I am most willing to have you, if you will have me. I desire to twist our lives together so tightly they can never be untangled."

"Your desire is true to your name," she murmured.

"But Freeblade will gladly have you too," he hastened to say, "though he knows that you would never have his whole heart. We spoke together, and he gave me his blessing to make this offer."

"And if I say no?" she asked almost too softly to be heard.

He swallowed. "I will love you anyway, and leave you alone, and say nothing to anyone but Freeblade. And should I find a man of power worthy of you, I will bring him to you at once."

"Then I would be a fool to say no."

Binder could not fasten onto her words. "Are you saying . . . ?"

"Don't you know *yes* when you hear it?" she asked lightly. "Of course I will."

"But are you truly willing to forfeit the cure?" he asked hesitantly. "You need a man of power—and I have less than any other man in this house. Wordsmith. Lionheart. Free-blade, again. And if Covenant wanted to free you, he would have done so already. I, on the other hand, have only a few battered books and a legacy of orphans to look after. If you accept me, you are doomed to a different face every day for-ever."

"Binder," she said softly, "I would rather be joined to a man with no power who cares for me than to a powerful man who is not knit to me and acts only for pity's sake. It is *you* who must pay the price of having *me*. Can you love and live with a woman you can recognize only by her cloak?"

"Whenever I close my eyes, you are the same woman I hear every day and have come to know."

"Then close your eyes now."

He complied. She took his hands in hers and brought them up to her face. "Feel very carefully," she requested. Binder gladly and gently explored her face with his fingers. "Would you know that face again if you felt it?"

"I would."

"Now look at me. Do I look the same as the last time your eyes were open?"

"No," he said. "But I have come to expect that."

"Close your eyes again, and touch my face. Is it different or the same?"

"The same," he said excitedly.

"I hoped it would be," she sighed happily. "Can you be con-tent with that? My touch and my loyalty are the only constant gifts I can offer you."

"I am more than content," Binder said. "I am well satisfied."

They held each other and ignored Glory beneath them.

I'm not sure who made the first offer, Binder thought, *or who made this final decision.*

* * *

"You are a noble man, Binder," said Freeblade, after the two walkers returned to the house and announced their pact.

"Blessed be the two of you, and the boys as well, as you begin to fight the wonderful battle of hearts entwined. I have another battle to fight tomorrow; I thank you for clearing my burdens that I can fight with an undivided heart and an undistracted mind."

Covenant blessed them as well, asking them, "Is there any reason to wait?"

"This is not a certain time," said Binder. "Freeblade must fight tomorrow, and even you seem weighed with woes."

Covenant nodded sadly. "My thoughts are, indeed, heavy for the coming day. But it is fully fitting to begin a marriage on the eve of battle. Let love run its course even in the face of war. Many will strive to be named King tomorrow; let us crown you a king tonight, and usher you into your own kingdom."

And so there was a third marriage in that house, with Covenant presiding and binding the two together as husband and wife. Binder's pledge, already fashioned in secret hope, was large and hollow, and it unscrewed into two pieces. It swallowed up the medallion on her pledge of punishment and closed tightly to hide it from the world forever.

"You may still be cursed," said Binder tenderly, "but you shall not wear your badge of shame openly."

*　*　*

The next morning Beauty and Wordsmith were surprised to see Binder seeking Covenant before breakfast. There was a fire in his eyes and a light in his heart, and he said only, "I have a question for him that will not wait."

He eventually found Covenant on a balcony, being warmed by the rising sun, and confronted him affectionately. "Covenant," he challenged, "tell me again the cure for chameleon."

"A man of power must marry her and undo the curse."

"Then what happened last night?" demanded Binder.

Covenant turned the question around. "What happened last night, Binder?"

124

He sought for the right words, and began. "We slept, and woke early, and she bore a face I had never seen before. She has had that same face now for hours."

Covenant smiled, and beckoned him to a seat. "And do you think she has been freed?"

"I believe so, but cannot prove it."

"You seem both certain and confused," observed Covenant.

"I am certain of what I see; I wonder if others will see the same thing."

"There is one way to know."

"Yes," said Binder. "Will you join us for her entrance?"

"Gladly," said Covenant.

* * *

The entire company was assembled when Binder led his lady into the room. They saw her shining face and expectant smile as she gazed at each of them in turn.

"What manner of woman do you see?" she asked Beauty directly.

"I see a woman with black hair and blue eyes and creamy skin," she said.

"So do I," said Wordsmith with surprise.

"And I," added Candle.

"And I," confirmed Moonflower.

"As do I," concluded Freeblade.

She turned her eyes to Covenant. "I want to believe that I am freed, but I do not know how it was done. Is this your work?"

"No," said Covenant, "it was done by the two of you."

"But you said it could be done only by a man of great power."

"Only a man could do it," responded Covenant, "but you misunderstood what power is. Power is not only might to hammer the world into the shape you please, but is also the privilege of changing the outside of another from the inside out, with power and persuasion and commitment. He has loved you with the selfless love he has found in this house, and your return of his love multiplied his power. Both of you made a sacrifice of hope born of hope, and your offerings combined to kindle a magic greater than that of any mighty man."

"Then you are no longer the Chameleon Lady," said Beauty. "What shall we call you?"

Everyone looked to Covenant, who extended his palm to Binder and left it to him.

"If it is, indeed, up to us," said Binder, "we would have her called Lady Brightface."

"It is well, and it is done," pronounced Covenant.

All the company applauded, and they beheld her true face at length before Binder led her away again to their room. She was neither remarkable nor wretched, but the love Covenant had poured into her heart—and confirmed there by Binder—transformed her, and none who saw her that day would ever forget her.

SEVENTEEN

Blood
and
Valor

WHEN THE SUN ROSE HIGHER, THE COMPANY OF COVENANT left the house behind and mingled with the growing crowd descending on the amphitheater.

There Freeblade took his place in the long line and waited his turn to throw in the metal marker with his name on it. Having done so, he announced his challenge: "Freeblade— Champion of the House of Covenant."

Covenant and his followers applauded him and cheered; few others did so—not of disdain, or favoritism, but because most were too afraid to cheer anyone just yet.

The tournament preparations continued with the drawing of markers, and the solemn painting of the ranks of the opponents' names on the wall that surrounded the amphitheater.

"Their names mean nothing to me," murmured Freeblade, fingering the grip of his sword. "I know none of them."

"They know nothing of you," returned Covenant. "But mark this name: Fame. You will see him slay many, for he has long awaited this chance."

"Fame." Freeblade studied the names and the lines on the wall. "Our names are on opposite ends, so he would be my ultimate opponent—if both of us survive so long."

"Yes," said Covenant. "He is the first contender on that side, and he will also be the final contender of those names."

"It will be my highest pleasure to slay your old enemy," swore Freeblade.

"That is what I feared," said Covenant, smiling again to take away any offense.

And at noon the tournament master opened the arena for the fighting.

Fame was first onto the hot sand, first to unsheathe his sword, first to brandish his emblazoned shield for the crowd.

Brightface began to moan, and clung tightly to Binder. "It's him!" she whispered fiercely. "The magic man! The one who cursed me! I did not know it was Fame!"

Binder nodded his head sadly and hid her face against his shoulders. "I am not surprised. His hand seems to be found in anything dark."

In the arena Fame raised his sword with a smile and beckoned his opponent closer to him. Fame struck first, and often, and last, and never swung his sword without a smile.

And when he had felled his foe, Fame dipped his hand in his opponent's blood and struck the dead man's name from the wall.

The sorrowed supporters carried the body away.

The next two combatants came promptly to the center of the arena, touched their swords together, and began their dance of death. Brutality began to replace formality, as hatred and greed and naked desire conquered ceremony and left it bleeding in the dust.

All Glory watched in horrified fascination as the tournament wound its bloody way down the length of the walls. Many of those who raised their sword in victory were themselves cut down by harder blows.

"Traditions die hard," said Covenant, "but so must many men. Every weapon that a man can make will be twisted back upon him and pierce him through the heart.

"But take courage," he continued, "for your sword was not made by human hands, and you shall not fight with human strength.

"You must fight fiercely," he said to the restlessly pacing Freeblade, "yet with mercy. When you have knocked your man to the ground, and he fails to rise again, you must offer him the chance to withdraw with his life."

"But the rules are to kill or be killed," objected Freeblade.

"That is what the people expect. I have told you what *I* expect of you."

"What if they do not take the offer, but fight on?"

"They will accept your offer," Covenant smiled, "and do so gladly. Slay no one—but defeat them roundly."

The excitement of the crowd began to turn into subdued and horrified awe. Most there had seen death before, but never so violent, so frequent and so deliberate. Yet death held sway, holding hands with victory, until Freeblade's name was called and he met his first challenger.

Thrust, parry, block and swing. His foe was older and more clever, but Freeblade was quicker and stronger, and the fire of Covenant's charter burned in his eyes. He was a man who would not be denied.

Time and time again he struck with the flat of the blade, wearing away where he could have slashed and skewered. His opponent was not so kind, and soon opened a crimson line along Freeblade's arm. Freeblade looked surprised, and glanced at Covenant, but then redoubled his efforts; in only a moment more one of his strokes shivered the challenger's shield, and his opponent stumbled backward and lay stunned.

Freeblade laid the tip of his sword against his opponent's throat. "Do you accept defeat?" shouted Freeblade.

"Yes," groaned his opponent weakly, expecting the fatal thrust.

"Then go," Freeblade ordered. "Your wounds are not mortal, and I do not seek your head as a trophy. You are not my enemy," he continued, "you are only my opponent. This fight is over; take your sword and go." Then, after a moment's thought, Freeblade smeared his fingers in his own blood and walked to the wall to strike out his opponent's name.

Trueteller and Lionheart tended his wound while Free-blade's eyes searched Covenant's face in puzzlement.

"I did not promise you would be unharmed," said Covenant. "I only said that you would not be defeated."

They watched Fame conquer again. "You will not have to face him," promised Covenant.

"Will he fall in combat?" asked Freeblade. "I do not see how he can."

"He will not lose. And neither will you," stated Covenant.

"But I must face him for the right to fill the throne."

"No. You will be spared that."

"I do not understand."

"You need not understand. You are a warrior? Then fight, and leave the wisdom to others."

Freeblade saluted him gravely with the sword and turned again to watch the fighting.

The list grew smaller—by death and also by withdrawal. Many of Fame's foes withdrew; few of Freeblade's challengers did so, seeing that they risked defeat at his hands but not death.

So Fame fought viciously and hungrily, but against fewer and fewer opponents, while Freeblade fought on longer under the sun.

"It is easy to kill a man," mumbled Freeblade to Covenant between matches. "It is far harder *not* to kill him while winning."

"You are learning the value of controlled wrath," said Covenant, "and they are learning lessons of their own. Blood means little to them until it is time to spill their own."

When the final light of day fell from the sky, only two were left to strive for the crown. "Enough!" cried the tournament master. "Let these two not meet until the sun has come to us again!"

But Fame could not leave without taunting the exhausted Freeblade. Ignoring Covenant and the rest, he spat to the warrior, "Go home and lick your wounds, my ambitious friend. You will need your strength for tomorrow!"

Though the fighting was postponed, bets were still taken briskly long after darkness fell.

At the house, Covenant tended Freeblade's many wounds himself. "Each fight has cost you a price of blood," said Covenant, "and you will have these scars forever."

"Then I will wear them proudly," answered Freeblade, and then fell asleep.

But Freeblade's arm stiffened during the night, and a low fever that began after midnight raged high in his body by dawn.

The others gathered around him, concerned and puzzled.

"Covenant, why do you not heal Freeblade?" whispered Wordsmith.

"Sudden health is not always the best road to wholeness," answered Covenant.

"But I cannot fight like this!" moaned Freeblade.

"No, you cannot," said Covenant simply. "The rules of the tournament hold that a champion who is not defeated but cannot continue may be replaced by another of his company."

"Then let me fight," offered Binder, and Brightface gripped his arm in fear. "By your hand I have rescued my lady from

Fame, and it is only fitting that I should avenge her as well."

"Vengeance is not the need of the moment," said Covenant kindly, "or I would accept your offer gladly."

Brightface relaxed again.

"Men you may face, Freeblade," Covenant continued, "and against men you may prevail; your battles yesterday were against flesh and blood. But Fame is not altogether flesh, nor is it altogether blood that pounds in his veins. You may not fight him. You would not win, and even if you could win you would be forced to win the wrong way. I must win *my* way, else all will be lost."

And then the company realized that Covenant would take the sword himself. They were wounded by the thought of Covenant suffering, and they could not imagine him fighting, but neither could they imagine him losing. All of them—including Binder and Brightface, and the wounded warrior who would not stay in bed—followed him silently to the area where the restless crowd and eager challenger awaited them.

"I will still fight for you, if you only give the command," whispered Freeblade to Covenant.

"You would not prevail."

"But I would die proudly!" insisted Freeblade.

Covenant shook his head. "It is not your day to die."

"Then take my feeble blessing as protection while you fight for the throne."

"You misunderstand me," said Covenant. "I do not fight for me. *I* am fighting now as *your* champion—and not that I may be crowned King of Glory." He smiled a sad smile, and said, "I am already King—though none but you few will acknowledge it."

"Then take my weapons," urged Freeblade. "This sword and shield have served me well."

"I need no weapons," said Covenant, returning Freeblade's offerings with a bow and the honor of a hovering smile. Then he strode into the center of the arena unarmed.

EIGHTEEN

The Judgment Stone

W HO ARE YOU?" THE MASTER SHOUTED TO THE BEGGAR. "Where is this Freeblade?"

"I am Covenant," the beggar called loudly enough for all to hear. "I am here because Freeblade is weak and fevered, and cannot fight this day. I have come to fight as champion for the champion of my house."

When Fame saw that Covenant had come to fight, and was unarmed, he threw down his own shield and gripped his sword before him with his hands clasped together. "You are a fool," Fame sneered to his old enemy, "to come against me at all, and a fool many times over to come against me with your bare hands."

The tournament master waved his hands and stepped back, and Fame rushed recklessly at Covenant, his sword dancing its deadly dance in the air.

But Covenant slipped beneath the flicking blade and tripped Fame.

Fame rose again, his face smeared with dust and contorted with anger.

Covenant stood his ground, and turned away yet another leap with surprising agility.

It was not the fight the crowd expected. Covenant did not press the attack, but continued standing firm and eluding most of Fame's lunges. Widening stripes of blood began to appear on Covenant's arms, yet still he stood unbroken. The crowd had begun to jeer Fame now, for being unable to dispatch an unarmed street beggar. Fame's arms were growing heavy, and he realized he would tire sooner than the unburdened and still nimble Covenant.

He threw the sword down in frustration and leaped upon the beggar with long fingers like talons. Across and around the arena they wrestled, Fame clawing and tearing, while Covenant broke hold after hold. They fought grimly, and for the first time the company saw Covenant suffer in open agony. He seemed to be dying; his flesh was bruised in countless places, his clothes and skin were badly torn, and blood still flowed from the evil cuts.

Fame knocked Covenant down with a stunning kick, and the beggar could rise only to his knees. Fame stumbled up steps to the Stone of Judgment and braced himself to crush his enemy from its heights. "I defy you," he howled. "You are wounded and winded, and cannot rise to fight me." He stamped his feet—and the rock beneath him suddenly began to crumble. He jumped back desperately and found solid footing just as the massive flattened peak of the stone split from its base and thundered down upon Covenant with a horrific smash.

The Stone embedded itself in the ground, leaving no sign of the beggar beneath.

All Glory stared in shock at the abrupt ending. Fame gazed down with glazed eyes, his utter surprise turning quickly into triumph.

The company of Covenant was frozen, stunned, until

Freeblade drew his weapon and stumbled screaming to the fallen rock. He began to dig frantically in the sand with his sword, and the others of the company were right behind him. A few of the crowd joined them in their efforts, but the rest of the people held back. Some, maddened by the lust for blood, cheered Fame wildly. Most were silent and uncertain.

An hour passed as they dug frantically. Glory waited impatiently and Fame grinned, savoring the moment he knew must come. Some in the crowd looked at Fame's face and began to regret their earlier cheers.

At last the rescuers undermined the side of the stone, and with the dregs of their strength tipped the slab sideways into the hasty pit.

The beggar was not there. Beneath the rubble there was only his cloak, drenched with drying blood and pounded deep by the falling rock. More blood had soaked deep into the sand and turned it a dark reddish-brown.

"No man could shed this much blood and live!" shouted one of the helpers.

Wordsmith stood by the ugly stain and gazed up at the triumphant Fame. "By this blood," he thundered, "you have sealed your own death!"

Fame gazed coldly down upon him, and said, "I shall deal with your sorry group shortly—and efficiently." Then he roared to the crowd, "Is there anyone left to challenge me?"

There was only silence in response.

"Then I claim the crown of Glory!" he declared. Silence met his pronouncement, and only slowly did the cheers begin to rise. Then more joined, until all but a few in the crowd acknowledged him and honored him with their praise. He immediately began to call out names, appointing advisors and captains and men-at-arms.

The company had no heart for the ceremonies. They gathered up the bloody cloak and returned home silently.

NINETEEN

The Death
of the
Dream

IN THE END THERE WAS NO TRUE BURIAL. AT WORDSMITH'S suggestion, Covenant's cloak (stiff now with his blood) was hidden deep within the walls of the house he had rebuilt for them. Candle placed it in a carved stone chest taken from his own special treasures. They were sad beyond words.

They huddled around Wordsmith the steward, hungry for some words from him and for the warmth of the only fire they had the interest to light.

"He warned us of this," said Wordsmith. "He said this would happen. He told us, but we did not understand it until now."

"Why didn't he tell us this directly?" moaned Beauty. "He *knew* this was going to happen."

"Perhaps we would have interfered if we had understood his words," said Wordsmith. "But he did leave us with wisdom and with promises. Covenant took me into the desert, and there he told me many things that I did not understand and still cannot fathom. Though I did not see the wisdom of it until now, at his bidding I wrote down his every word." His fingers smoothed the new leather on the tiny book he produced from his pouch. "These are his words to me, as nearly as I could snatch them from the air. Who can fully capture the truth that Covenant speaks? You must find a greater writer than I for that . . . but these will do, these will have to do.

"When Covenant . . . vanished, it seems that my eyes were opened to many things that he said—as if he were speaking words into my mind, and not simply leaving them on paper. I have words of hope you must hear. Covenant made provisions. Hear, now, what he gave me to give to you.

"He told me that he would soon go where we could not find him, and that he would not leave us in our sorrow but would send another in his place. He told me that when I sought him in vain, I should go and seek for the Child Upon the Mountain."

"A child?" asked Beauty.

"*The* Child," corrected Wordsmith.

"Which mountain?" asked Freeblade—even as his eyes turned toward Lonely Mountain.

"The mountain where few have ever ventured," Wordsmith replied, "and from which none has ever returned."

"What shall *we* find there?"

"The Child," Wordsmith said, "but I know no more than that. How could a child survive the deep snows and icy storms that rage atop that mountain?"

"How shall we get up, and how we shall we find him, and how we shall we get down again?" asked Freeblade.

Wordsmith shrugged his shoulders. "I do not know. Perhaps we will discover that when we get there."

"This all seems so remote now," murmured Binder. "Was he ever really here? Was he only a ghost?"

"If he was only a ghost, then where did the blood come from?" responded Brightface, squeezing his hand ever tighter.

"If anything," said Wordsmith, "he is more real to me now than when he was with us. He was always coming and going, and I did not know when I would see him, but now I feel as though he is standing at my side. I cannot explain it, but I am reassured by this invisible presence even in my numbness and grief."

After a long silence, Freeblade spoke again. "But what must we do now? Do we sit here and wait? Do we leave for the mountain immediately?"

"No," answered Wordsmith, "I am afraid we must all leave this place. Fame is gathering his soldiers, and I do not think he will be long in hunting us down."

"How do you know that?" challenged Candle. And then, more softly, "I do not mean to anger you, but I do not know what to do. I do not know if we even should follow you from this house—which is strong and sure. Did he not build it with his own hands?"

Wordsmith answered quietly. "I have just come from the tower he built for me. The four windows are black—dead or dying or dimmed—and the fifth window is an ugly swirl of clouds that reveals nothing.

"And I have tested the Door to the City. This key will no longer open it." He paused. "The heart has gone from this house."

Even through their numbing shock they could sense the growing chill of the silent stones, and they knew that the cold creeping into their bones was not born solely of their own fear.

"I do not claim that any of you should follow me," said Wordsmith. "But I will do what I feel must be done, and the rest of you are free to follow if you wish."

"It is only a building," said Brightface sadly, "now that Covenant is gone."

"We cannot defend this place against Fame's men," Free-blade stated. "I am with Wordsmith, for I know of Covenant's deep regard for him—and Fame's hatred for us all."

"And I am with you," said Beauty, "though I should not need to say so."

"And so are we," Binder said. Brightface, leaning her head against Binder's arm, added, "I cannot live my life in the presence of Fame."

"But I cannot go," said Lionheart, "without my charges. And where will we hide? Must I take my infants and elderly out into the wilderness?"

"Here is my counsel," said Wordsmith. "Let us all go to the one place where no one will ever go again—Heartbreak, the village of the lepers. It is empty, even though there are houses there, and a well, and a forest beyond for food. I think," he added, smiling, "that Lionheart could readily make it feared as a place of lions and other fierce beasts."

"Should I shutter my shop as well?" asked Candle.

"Perhaps—and perhaps not," answered Wordsmith. "You are not as dependent on this house as we are, and though you came early you are not widely known to be among our company. If you are willing to run the risk, it might be very useful if you moved back into your shop and stayed in Glory."

Candle looked at Moonflower. "She will find it hard to flee far now. I will go back to my shop and stay in Glory. Trueteller may make her own decision."

"Will you have me if I stay?" she asked her son-in-law.

"Of course," he said. "You bring light to our house—and you are neither a burden nor a busybody."

"Is there anyone else who wishes to stay?" asked Word-smith.

No one answered.

"The soldiers will be looking for us," said Wordsmith. "Let us go from this place quickly."

"But how shall we get to Heartbreak?" asked Freeblade.

"Lionheart's children cannot run all the way."

"My lions will come and carry us," said Lionheart. "But I fear there are not enough lions to bear all of us at once."

"There is a large wagon standing ready at the gates," said Beauty quietly. "It was given to us as we returned from the sea, but I did not imagine we would have need of it. It is a poor cart, but we must use what we have been given."

"Not even Roadreeler and Kingsburro together can pull that ancient wreck," said Freeblade.

Wordsmith looked about him in the shadow of defeat, but Lionheart spoke again. "Perhaps the others will help as well. When Covenant . . . died, part of his power fell upon you. Perhaps another part of it has fallen upon me. Go and pick what you can carry, and I will see what I can do."

They packed in haste, wrapping food and gathering the animals. By ones and twos, they quietly left the roar of Glory and assembled outside the gates. The elderly, the infants and the infirm were loaded on the wagon, along with the few belongings they had salvaged. Freeblade refused to ride upon the wagon, even though his wounds had not yet healed.

"Now, Lionheart," said Wordsmith, "where is our help?"

Lionheart opened his mouth and rent the air with the roar of a lion, and no one was surprised. Then he added the growl of a bear, and the howl of a wolf, and finally the bracking bray of a stag, and they stared at him.

All came—lions, bears, wolves and deer—to stand in the shadow of the trees and await further words from Lionheart. He beckoned eight of the shaggy black bears, who shuffled over to him and huffed noisily in the air as he adjusted the worn harnesses about them.

"We can go now," said Lionheart. "The bears are swifter than you think, and strong and sure. The lions will carry the rest of us, and the wolves and deer will guard our way and cover our tracks behind us." He reached his hand out in wonder to stroke the shaggy head beside him. "I have only begun to understand the privilege that has been given me."

"Let us go then," said Wordsmith. Lionheart spoke, and the bears lurched off with the load. The others each mounted a lion, not without misgivings, and they slipped away from Glory with regret, pain and many a backward glance.

* * *

King Fame and his soldiers reached the house of Covenant only to find it abandoned.

"I am not surprised that they have scattered," said Fame. "Take what you please from the house," he ordered, "and then pull the stones down. Leave no trace that the beggar and his kind were ever here."

"Should we search for them?" asked his captain. "They are your enemies."

"There is no hurry now," said Fame, dismissing the suggestion with a wave of his hand. "Let them go, and let their god be forgotten again and forever. There are more urgent tasks to be done than chasing vermin. Their house has once again fallen, for they have no leader and no path to follow. Let them go where they will, for they cannot hide long from my wrath. They are fools fleeing in fear, and there is no place for them in Glory."

── TWENTY ──

Heartshope

T HE COMPANY LEFT THE MAIN ROAD AND CREAKED TOWARD Heartbreak moments before the earthquake struck. The earth rippled and bucked and cracked while Lionheart struggled to hold the bears steady. The earthquake was sharp and strong and frightening, and it ended as suddenly as it started.

When they opened their eyes again, the land had stopped shaking, and the silence was immense.

Wordsmith gestured at the field beside them. "Many people are buried here," he said. "But look—the earthquake has ruined even the graves."

Freeblade dismounted stiffly and cautiously explored the upheaval. Some of the graves were sunken where the mounded earth had collapsed, and some of the tombs were broken apart. "Have wild animals taken the bones already?" he called. "The broken tombs are empty."

Only some of the graves had been disturbed, and Wordsmith could see no pattern to the disorder.

Binder pointed over the hill. "But what about the greater mystery? Is the village still standing?" They pressed on without answer to their questions.

*　*　*

Wordsmith's caravan halted in the middle of the deserted village, where mist and smoke still lingered on the ground.

Freeblade took his sword in his tired arms and searched the houses. "There seems to be no deep damage here," he said at last. "Unload the wagon."

It was mostly empty when they heard it creak and groan and splinter, and then it collapsed in a welter of worn wood and failed fittings.

Wordsmith stood and looked at the wooden ruins. "That which we cannot use in the buildings may at least become an honest fire," he said. "We owe the gift that much honor, at least."

Wordsmith kindled the fire as the others chose houses and stored away their pitifully few goods. Then, unsummoned, the Company filled their hands with food and gathered around the flames. Wearied by their grief and unplanned labors, they were grateful for a rest and listened long to the songs of the birds and beetles and other night musicians.

Beauty finally broke the spell of the silence. "Wordsmith," she said gently, "I cannot live in a place called Heartbreak. Cannot we give it another name? Covenant would have done so."

"What do you suggest?" asked Wordsmith.

"Why not Heartshope?" she proposed. "It is all we have left."

"It is good in my eyes," he replied. "Do the rest of you agree?" They nodded silently. "It is done, then," he continued, "and it is fitting for what I have to say."

He paused, searching for the right words. "I have not told you the most puzzling thing of all," he began, "though it is perhaps the most heartening thing as well. It is a word of comfort not from Covenant, but about him."

He looked carefully at their expectant faces. "Were any of you watching Covenant's face when the stone fell?" Wordsmith's eyes questioned each of them in turn, without result. "I had hoped one of you had seen him, too, and would add your voice to my story.

"I beheld his face," he continued, "even as he was overshadowed by his death. He was looking up, with his arms spread wide—not in fear, but in welcome.

"And he was smiling."